PLEATS & POISON

A CRAFT AND GHOST COZY MYSTERY

A DRESS DESIGNER COZY MYSTERY SERIES
BOOK 3

LUCINDA RACE

MC TWO PRESS

Editor Purple Pen Wordsmithing
Cover design by Molly Burton of Cozy CoverDesigns.com

Manufactured in the United States of America
First Edition August 2025

Print Edition ISBN 978-1-966424-38-3
Amazon Print Edition ISBN 979-8-294835-22-4

E-book ISBN 978-1-966424-37-6

1. Town Hall
2. Lillith Park
3. Grants Gowns
4. Whistlers Inn
5. Twice Loved
6. DB Pharmacy
7. Drakes Bay Bank
8. Police Department
9. Knit or Purl
10. 5 Cents a Dance
11. Polly's Pantry
12. Brewed Bliss
13. Blossoms on the Bay
14. Scoop-a-licious

1

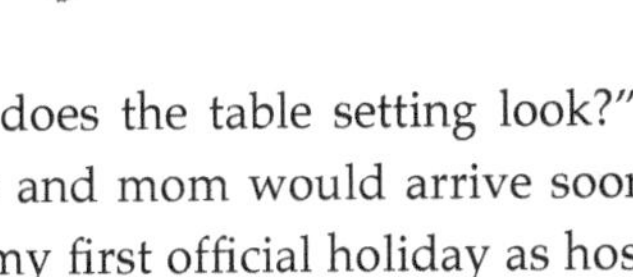

"Herman, how does the table setting look?" My grandmother and mom would arrive soon for Thanksgiving. As this was my first official holiday as hostess, butterflies tickled my insides. Uncle Herman, my resident ghost, drifted in from the kitchen.

"Why did you have to set up a table right in front of my window seat? Whoever sits there will block my view. I like to watch people stroll down Cade Street after the Turkey Trot is finished."

Groaning, I hung my head. "This is my first major holiday in Drakes Bay, and my family is coming to stay for a few days. Could I get a little support?"

"They're my family, too. Not that we'll be able to catch up about the old days, but still, I'll have the opportunity to see them at least."

"There's the right attitude." My arm swept over the table. "What do you think? The dishes were a find at Twice Loved and they're perfect, don't you agree?"

"I've said it before. Fiona has impeccable taste. I'm glad

you invited her, and Beth, Ethan, and Eddie too. What time is our family arriving?"

"In a little over an hour. Mom called and said they were making excellent time coming up 95, and there's very little traffic. I've got the turkey in the oven, and the veggies are ready to cook. Beth is bringing dessert, and Ethan said his contribution would be a surprise."

Herman floated around the table. "What about the wine?"

A small smile played over my mouth. "Eddie offered to help me pick out the wine for dinner from your stash."

"Harrumph. If you keep sampling from the wine cellar and don't add to it soon, it will dry like a withered grape left on the vine after harvest." He perched on the window ledge. "Speaking of your favorite police officer, he's crossing the street now and seems to be headed to your alley."

I hurried across the room and peered out. Eddie glanced up and waved. My cheeks flushed as he caught me looking out the window at him. "Maybe he wants to…"

Moments later a sharp knock on the back door had me running a hand down the front of my apron before I tore it off and tossed it over the chair.

My ghost chuckled. "You look spiffy."

"Not what I was going for." I walked leisurely to the back entrance, hoping I appeared casual and not at all like my heart thumped wildly in my chest.

Eddie grinned as I opened the door. "Come in."

"Gigi, hey. I hope you don't mind that I dropped by early." He held out a bouquet. "These are for you. I wasn't sure if you'd want them on the table or someplace else, but my mom always had flowers for every holiday."

My heart skipped a beat when he used his special nickname for me. I brought them to my nose and inhaled. The fragrant apricot roses, lavender, and freesia would be perfect for the table. "Thank you. That's a sweet tradition." I shut the door. "I didn't expect you. Please don't say you have to work."

"Not this year. Rhonda Perkins has the day shift, and I'm not on evenings or nights this month."

"Lucky you." I smiled, unsure why he was three hours early. I asked, "Would you like a cup of coffee?"

He chuckled, reached out a finger, and wiped my cheek. "Breadcrumbs. No, thanks. I've had enough caffeine for today. We could choose the wine for dinner. Unless you're busy?"

I liked how he answered me with a question. He wasn't as self-assured when it came to whatever was going on between us. When he was in his police uniform, he oozed confidence.

"I have time. My mom and grandmother won't be here for at least another hour. They're driving through Portland. Mom texted, saying it would take that long per the GPS, and she follows it to the exact minute."

A mischievous twinkle hovered in his blue-grey eyes. "She's not a rule breaker like her daughter?"

I knew he was referring to my help solving two murders we had in town… Well, and an assault. "Hey, I don't break rules. I just see if they're at all flexible."

"Is that what you're calling it when you put yourself in danger with criminals?"

Giving him a friendly punch on the arm, I walked into the kitchen. "It's not my fault the police department needed an objective eye on their cases."

Herman called from his perch. "Vases are in the pantry closet, top shelf."

"Would you mind grabbing me a vase? They're on the top shelf in the cabinet."

I removed the flowers from the protective film and trimmed the ends while Eddie filled the vase he had chosen with water. After arranging the flowers and after my heart returned to a normal rhythm, I placed them in the center of the dining table. "They're perfect."

He cleared his throat. "About the wine?"

"Right. We're having seven people for dinner. I mean, seven people are coming to dinner." My cheeks burned, hoping he missed the word, *we're*. It sounded like *we* were hosting.

"We should select two different varieties and bring up four bottles, two whites and two reds."

I flipped the lock on the door that led into my dress shop and turned on the overhead light. "Earlier, I was thinking about the wine cellar. I'm going to need to restock at some point. Would you want to visit a few of the wineries this winter and help me select some vintages? I'm sure Beth and Luke would want to come." I deliberately kept it casual, like four friends getting together to have fun.

Herman didn't drift by us as we descended the stairs. The shop was dark except for the soft lighting illuminating the display windows and a desk lamp.

"Once they post the December schedule, I can let you know what Sundays I'm off, and we can plan it."

"Great, it's a date." *Date? Really? Once again, open your mouth and insert your foot.* I tugged the bolt of fabric that hid the basement door, hoping he wouldn't notice my cheeks likely flaming to a deep holiday red.

With the door open I hurried down the steps, pausing to flick on the lights in the main room. Every time I looked at the theatre room Herman had built, I was awestruck. "My uncle had a great sense of style."

"This is a fantastic space." He waited while I entered the utility room before following me into the wine cellar. "It's easy to see he put thought into the entire building."

Would Herman appear as he usually did when I came downstairs? I glanced around the space, but we were alone. Eddie was holding a bottle of white wine. "Sweet or oaky."

"Definitely oaky. I wonder, should we bring up a dessert wine too?"

With a lopsided grin, he said, "It's your wine cellar and you're the hostess. Whatever you want."

A nervous laugh escaped. "Sometimes I forget this is all mine and I'm not a guest."

His face softened. "I'm glad you came to town. Life has been so much more interesting since you arrived."

"Um. Thanks?"

His fingers grazed the air between us as if offering reassurance. "That was a compliment."

"Good. Then, thank you. Now, about the wine."

We selected six bottles: four for dinner and two for dessert. Before taking the stairs, he paused on the bottom step. "Maybe sometime we could watch a movie?"

My heart skipped again. "I'd like that."

"Then it's an almost plan." He swept his arm in front of me. "After you."

*E*ddie took care of the wine before he left. I closed the oven after basting the turkey hoping it would be flavorful and juicy. Like my one hit wonder, macaroni and cheese, this was the best holiday dinner I could prepare, and I wanted my grandma to be impressed. Mom was less concerned about what we ate than about being together. It needed to be a win in everyone's eyes.

"Claudia, what kind of car does your mother drive?" Herman asked.

I closed the oven door. "A black sedan."

"One's pulled up in front of the store."

I slipped on a jacket, burst out the door, and raced down the back steps. It had been ten months since I had seen my family in person, and it wasn't until this exact moment that I realized how much I missed them.

Running with my arms wide, I cried, "Mom. Gram."

They enveloped me in a hug and held me tight.

"Claudia, it's so good to see you," Mom said.

"I'm thrilled you're here." I pecked Grandma's cheek. "Both of you."

She brushed my hair back behind my ear. "Your hair's gotten so long. You didn't have time for a trim? And this pink streak? It's very noticeable in your blond hair."

"Oh, Grandma. I'm growing it longer, and I like it. The pink is to support breast cancer awareness month."

"I like it." Mom said, "It suits you." She looked over the building from the sidewalk to the roofline. "This is your everything? Home, work, social life?"

"It is, and I can't wait to show you every square inch. Uncle Herman created a lovely store, a comfortable home, and a few surprises, too."

I picked up their tote bags, slung one over each shoulder, and said, "Follow me."

"You mentioned you have friends joining us for dinner?" Mom gasped as we reached the bottom of the stairs. "Is that the ocean?"

Grandma rushed to the edge of my parking area. "Herman said it was a nice view, but I had no idea."

"Gram, why didn't you ever come and visit him? He had a spare room."

Her smile slipped. "Herman insisted he come to us for family get-togethers, and when it wasn't a holiday, he was busy working. Your grandfather and I never wanted to intrude. But seeing this stunning view, I wish we had."

"Wait until you see it from the deck. At the end of a busy day, I sit and watch the water, and on occasion have drinks and dinner with friends." I gave them a few minutes to soak it all in before saying, "We should get upstairs. We can have tea before everyone arrives."

"Can we have tea on the deck? I can't stop looking at the ocean," Mom said.

"Yes. I kept the chairs out—at least until the first snow flies, which can be any day now according to Beth."

Their boots clomped as we climbed the stairs. Mom and Gram couldn't tear their eyes away from the Atlantic. Who knew they'd find it so captivating? I eased the door open, and Lola was sitting in the hall. She meowed in greeting, and Herman rested on the small bench.

"Is this Herman's cat?" Mom asked as she knelt to run her hand along the length of the feline's soft fur.

"Yes. Isn't she beautiful? And she's been a wonderful companion." I dropped the tote bags on the floor. "I'll show you to your rooms."

"Honey," Mom said, "We think it best to check into the inn tomorrow. It's right next door which is super convenient, and we've already made our reservations."

"That's not necessary. I've got it all worked out. Grandma has my room, and you have the spare room."

"Hey, that's my room." Herman zipped away. I didn't get the opportunity to remind him that he didn't sleep in a bed, and he never minded when Beth stayed over, especially when I first moved to town and was suspected of killing a local man.

"For one night." Gram patted my cheek. "Trust me, it will be better for us all. I snore like a freight train and your mom is a light sleeper."

Instead of arguing with them, I asked, "How about a tour of the apartment?" I linked arms with them and guided them into the main living space. "To the right is the kitchen, and that door leads to the shop, so I don't have to go outside to commute to work. Life is so much easier than when I lived in New York City. This is a breeze."

"Honey, the table's beautiful. Did your uncle have this dinnerware?"

"Mom, I bought the set from this sweet shop in town, Twice Loved. You'll meet Fiona today. She also found a rug for my bedroom and a few other odds and ends. You and Gram must check it out while you're here, as well as Knit or Purl. Beth has the best yarns."

"The flowers are pretty, Claudia."

"Thanks, Gram." Unsure why I didn't say that Eddie brought them earlier, I said, "Time to wrap up the tour with the bedrooms. My room is on the left." Lola slipped in the door first and hopped onto the bed, looking like the queen of Drakes Bay.

"Oh, my." Mom hurried to the expanse of windows with the ocean view. "You wake up to this every day?"

"I do. Herman had Fiona help him decorate the space."

Gram did a slow three-sixty turn. "It's perfect. You know, he called and asked what your favorite colors were, but I had no idea this would be the result."

Herman drifted into the room. "Erma looks the same."

"Dana, look. There's a connecting door to the bathroom. Very handy."

Mom opened the closet doors. "I'd die for a closet like this." She joined my grandmother in the bathroom.

"You can see why I'm comfortable here. I couldn't have designed this space any better."

"Is Herman's room this nice?" Mom asked.

I shook my head. "It has a view of Cade and Main Streets, and it's the smaller of the two rooms. Ethan said it was because he liked the street noise. After moving from the city, the town was a little quiet for him."

They checked out his room, and Mom said, "The entire apartment is charming. Can we see the store next?"

Excited to show them the rest of the place, I grinned. "Don't let Lola follow us. I like to keep her out of the shop in case she decides a garment I'm working on makes for a cozy place to nap."

"I can see where cat hair, no matter how soft, wouldn't be a bonus to a customer." Grandma patted the kitty's head and winked at Herman's ghost. "If Herman were standing in front of me, I'd give him a huge hug and thank him for creating a wonderful home for you."

Herman gave her a courtly bow. "It's nice to see you, Erma."

I gave Mom a side glance, but she didn't acknowledge him.

What the heck? My grandmother can see ghosts, too?

2

———

$\mathcal{A}$fter the store tour and the movie room, my mom and grandma sat in Adirondack chairs on the deck with a cup of tea, watching the water.

"This is heaven and the tea is delicious," Grandma said. "Is it another local business?"

"Yes, I bought it from the Cozy Nook Bookstore in Pembroke Cove. It's about thirty minutes from here. The owners, Lily Michaels's parents, have a tea business."

She sipped. "I'll need to pick some up while I'm here. Now, tell me who's coming to dinner and when do we need to start cooking?"

"You don't have to do a thing. It's under control. And as for my bonus family, Beth and her dad, Ethan; her cousin, Eddie; and Fiona, the owner of the second-hand shop I mentioned are joining us."

"We haven't had a full table in a long time." Gram's eyes twinkled over her teacup. "Darling girl, will you please give us the juicy tidbits on the town? There's nothing like local color."

"Grandma, I'm not a gossip." I wanted to say I didn't know anything, but I couldn't lie. Small towns bubbled with a humming grapevine.

She twirled her finger in the air. "You never said there wasn't any."

I stood. "The turkey needs basting."

She called after me, "Herman would share the salacious details."

"Erma." Mom's hushed tone seeped into that word.

I smiled and closed the door to the apartment.

Herman floated behind me. "Did you know Erma could see ghosts?"

"No, I didn't." I glanced over my shoulder. "Don't share stories with her about me. It's only a matter of time before she grills me about my love life."

He snorted. "Are you referring to the flirtation you have with Eddie? There's not much to tell. At least not yet. The two of you are tap dancing around each other like you've just met, and it's been months."

Turning away from my ghost, I muttered, "There's something to be said for taking any relationship slow." I opened the oven door and basted the bird.

"How does it smell?" Herman floated between me and the door. "Turkey dinner was always a favorite of mine."

My smile sagged. "I'm sorry, Herman. Maybe I shouldn't have hosted Thanksgiving."

"Nonsense." His translucent form straightened to what might have been his full height when he'd been alive. "This is your home more than mine, now. I want you to *live* your life to the fullest every day!"

I had never heard his voice as robust, and he added extra emphasis when he said *live*. "There's nothing I can do about today, but are you sure I shouldn't avoid gatherings in the future?"

"Claudia, I enjoy people coming over to enjoy a meal or watch a movie and share a glass of wine with you. It's like

I'm still able to mingle, too. I don't want you to curb living for what you think will spare my feelings."

He hovered in the doorway at the top of the store stairs. "There's one thing you *could* do for me…"

"Anything." I felt so guilty for things I had no control over that right now I'd do almost anything for Herman to be happy.

"Make plans with Eddie to have a movie night in your private theater, like a date, just the two of you. He's a good man, and even before you moved to Drakes Bay, I thought you and he would make a nice couple."

With a snort, I glanced his way. "Are you saying that you're matchmaking in your ghostly form?"

"What else do I have to look forward to? I promise I won't drift in to see how things are going. Your privacy will be my utmost concern."

"If that will make you happy after the holiday, I'll ask Eddie for a movie and pizza night."

"Good, now, don't forget to show your grandmother that ensemble you and Beth worked on—the one with the burgundy cable knit pullover and pleated skirt—the set you just finished."

"Why that outfit?"

"It suits her, and if she takes it home, it would be great advertising for Beth and your new line."

"You're right; the burgundy colors would be perfect with her rosy complexion. I'll wait until Beth's here, though. I want her to get the accolades she deserves." I smiled at him. "Thank you."

"For?"

"Despite your current situation, you've got an excellent head for business."

"My dear Gigi, the brain cells work even if I'm less solid than in years past." He faded through the door.

"Herman. Wait." I called after him, but he was gone. Why

hadn't I remembered it was during this time last year he had died? I should have been more sensitive. "I'm sorry." There was no way to know if he heard me, but I had to apologize.

Mom came around the corner. "Did you call out for help?"

I shook my head. "No. I was talking to myself."

She pursed her lips, but I wasn't sure if she believed me. "Should we come in now to help? Your friends will be arriving soon."

"That's a good idea. I need to get the veggies cooked and the potatoes mashed."

Her sad eyes locked on mine for what seemed like a minute but was mere seconds. "I'll let Erma know."

My cell rang, and it gave me an excuse to look away. "Hello?"

"Hey, Claudia. Dad and I are heading over, but I wanted to make sure you didn't need anything from my house."

With a laugh, I smiled into the phone, "I don't need a thing except friends with big appetites."

"We skipped breakfast, so I am ravenous—and you know Eddie is a bottomless pit."

"He is. When you get here, I want to show everyone our latest collaboration. I gave Mom and Grandma a tour of the shop but glossed over our joint venture. I can't do justice to your talent. We should share our plans with them while we're together."

"You can—you're being modest. But you know I'd love to tell your family every detail. Do either of them knit? I can open the shop for them this afternoon."

"We're not working today. Just spending time with the people we love and eating good food. But..." I thought of Herman's suggestion, and I'd honor it. "There's an outfit that would be perfect for my grandmother."

"Then, we can show it off and all the others, too. Maybe they'll have some fresh ideas we can incorporate into the spring collection."

Smiling into the phone again, I said, "Perfect. Come on over."

"See you in ten minutes." She was laughing as she hung up the phone.

I pressed the phone to my body, grateful for my move to this small town and the people I found who became my chosen family.

*M*om and Grandma were sitting in the living room when I heard the familiar *tap, tap, tap* on the door. "They're here." I stood and crossed the room. "Come in," I called out.

Before I could reach the door, I heard Ethan. "Beth, will you take the pies in? I'll get the rest from the car."

I rounded the corner. Beth grinned. "Happy Thanksgiving," she held up a two-tiered pie carrier. "I've got pie—pumpkin and lemon meringue. Dad knows lemon anything is your favorite. He went back to the car to get the dinner rolls, and the apple and mince pies."

I took the desserts and laughed. "We'll have more pie than people."

"There's only four but that does give a half pie to each person." She hung her coat up, revealing a lovely variegated sweater in rich fall hues. She twirled around. "What do you think? Could you pair this with some trousers or skirt for next fall?"

Nodding, I said, "I think we should, but we have two self-proclaimed fashionistas in the living room, so we'll get their opinion." I bobbed my head toward the kitchen. "Come on in, and I'll introduce you."

"I'll wait to get the door for Dad and be right behind you."

"Fine. I'll move a few things around in the fridge to get the lemon pie in there."

"Hey, Claudia. Here's an idea I've used a bunch of times.

Why don't we store them on the deck? It's cold enough and that will free up kitchen space."

That was an excellent solution as I thought about my tiny fridge and all the food that needed refrigeration. I reversed direction and Beth opened the door for me.

Ethan jogged up the steps with a cardboard box.

"Dad, we're leaving the pies out here until after dinner."

"Perfect solution. I wondered where we were going to put everything." He removed the pies and placed them on the table between two chairs. Ethan dragged out a small dining table I had stored against the building and set all the pies on it.

"They look delicious. Are these from Nikki Twing's kitchen?"

Ethan staggered back, pretending I'd plunged a dagger into his chest. "You wound me. These are my homemade contributions to dinner, including the yeast rolls."

I giggled. "I thought we agreed you were going to place an order. The last thing I wanted was for you to go to a lot of trouble."

"What can I say? You know I enjoy cooking, and these recipes are Beth's mom's." He briefly closed his eyes, his face sagged.

"Dad, thank you. I didn't know you used Mom's recipes."

He kissed her cheek. "It's like she's with us today—and it was Eddie's suggestion. I can't take the credit."

I stood on my tiptoes and brushed my lips against his cheek. "This is a lovely way to include Beth's mom."

She cleared her throat. "This isn't a day for sadness. Now, we should get out of the cold and meet Claudia's mother and grandmother. I'm sure they must be wondering what's happened to us."

We entered the apartment. The mouth-watering smell of turkey roasting greeted us. I'd been inside for so long, this was the first time I noticed how welcoming it was. "Mom, Gram? Beth and Ethan are here."

They rose to their feet as we entered the living room. "Ethan Stewart, my mother, Dana Grant, and my grandmother, Erma Grant."

He shook their hands. "I remember you both from Herman's funeral. It's a pleasure to see you today. Did you have a nice trip up?"

"We did, thank you," Mom said. "There was little traffic, so driving this morning was the right decision. I forgot how lovely Maine is this time of year."

"Other than chilly," Gram said, "the view of the water from the deck is breathtaking."

"Grandma, it's cold at home, too."

She frowned. "Give an old woman her opinion."

I turned in a circle. "Where's there an old woman?"

She swatted the air and grinned, "Fresh girl."

"Just like the other women in the Grant family."

"Ethan, I'd like to thank you for watching over Claudia since she's arrived in town. That business with Herman's death was distressing. After she told us that you and Beth were being supportive, it was easier for me not to jump in the car and race up here."

"Dana, she's become like a second daughter to me. Trust me when I say she's made good friends, and we all look out for each other."

My cheeks grew warm under his kind smile and words.

Herman drifted behind the group, nodding. "I told you that you could trust Ethan." It was a running commentary from my ghost.

My grandmother glanced his way, and her eyebrow quirked as she turned to me. "Claudia, earlier, you said there was an outfit you wanted to show your mom and me after Beth arrived?"

Thank goodness she hadn't referred to Herman's comment. "Yes." I crossed the kitchen, opened the door to the shop, and switched on the overhead light. "Ladies? Shall we?"

Ethan asked, "Mind if I tag along?"

Beth laughed. "Dad just loves fashion. And he's one of our knitters. He likes to be in the know about what Claudia and I are working on."

"Ethan, you knit?" Mom's voice held a hint of surprise.

"When my late wife was ill, I took it up since it was something I could do while sitting next to her bed as she slept. It seemed a natural fit as Beth had opened Knit or Purl. After I retired, she took pity on me. I started stocking shelves, handling the counter, and knitting. At that time, she had a small inventory of items to purchase, but since then, that has expanded with the new venture our daughters developed a couple of months ago."

I ushered them to the main salon, and my mom and grandma stood in the archway.

Mom said, "Claudia, this space is lovely. I know we saw it a bit earlier, but both times I've walked in, I'm struck by how it suits you."

"Thanks, Mom." I looked at the space through her eyes. The soft white billowy curtains graced the front window displays of ready-to-wear items on one side and a wedding gown and flower girl dress in the other window. "Have a seat and relax, and we'll show you the new line and the ensemble I think is perfect for Gram."

Ethan waved them to the sofa, and he sat on the chair.

From the rack, I took the plaid wool pleated skirt, and Beth selected the sweater from the table. We added them to the dress form, and I carried it to the middle of the room. "Ta-da. From the creation of Beth's needles, a burgundy Merino wool fine cable-knit pullover, and a wool skirt with a matching yarn-dyed, wrap-style front with pleats in the back and finished with an asymmetrical hem."

Gram clapped her hands together and gushed. "Darling girls, this is a beautiful outfit, and I must buy it."

"Don't you want to try it on first, Gram?"

"Oh, I want to try it on, but I'm buying it."

Mom laughed. "The easiest sale you've probably had this month."

"Grandma, it's my Christmas gift to you."

Beth nodded. "And the sweater is my gift, too."

Gram was on her feet. "I'm paying for it, or it won't leave the store in my possession."

I gave Mom a pleading look.

She shrugged. "How about I buy it as your gift? Maybe Claudia can give me the family discount?" She gave me a conspiratorial wink. Money wouldn't change hands today.

Gram looked between me and Mom. "You'll take your mother's money but not mine?"

I hugged her tight. "Gram, you've done a lot for me. Talking with Herman about me becoming his apprentice, signing this business and building over to me. I couldn't accept any money from you, but if you won't take the outfit without payment and Mom is happy to pull out her credit card, then we both benefit. You get this stunning outfit to show off to everyone you know."

Beth smiled. "Mrs. Grant?"

"Erma, my dear girl. We don't stand on formality in this family."

She tipped her head. "Erma, would you like to try on your outfit now or after dinner?"

"Best to do it now since afterward, I'll be so full that the buckles on the skirt won't close." With a laugh, she took the skirt and sweater from Beth and went into the dressing room. "Claudia, I trust you can alter it if necessary."

"Gram, I can alter it. But I know your measurements, and it should be a perfect fit."

I heard her snort from inside the dressing room. "Besides, pleats are very forgiving."

3

-----

*C*heerful people surrounded me at our makeshift Thanksgiving table, and the conversation flowed easily as we ate. As if we needed more desserts, Fiona contributed a gingerbread cream pie and a pumpkin cheesecake. Intently listening from his windowsill perch, Herman's translucent form glowed with happiness, despite his inability to join the festivities.

I scooped the last of the gingerbread cream filling off my plate. "This is so good, Fiona."

"It's an old family recipe. I've made it every year for Thanksgiving for, well, too many years to count."

Herman hovered over my shoulder. "She made this every year we shared the holiday. We used to do friends-giving at Ethan's before his wife passed on."

"It's one of my favorite pies and wonderful memories when we gathered at our home for dinner." Ethan patted his midsection. "I'm not sure I could eat another bite. Well, at least until it's time for a thick turkey sandwich and more pie later."

I laughed, enjoying the post-dinner haze with family and

friends. "We should move to the sofa and chairs to be more comfortable."

Mom, Grandma, Fiona, and Ethan moved to the cushy seats while Eddie stacked the dessert plates. "Claudia, you should relax. This meal was a lot of work and worth every second you toiled over the hot stove. I'll take care of clean up."

I placed my hand out to stop him. "You're my guest."

Under his breath—I was the only person to hear—he said, "Gigi, your family has driven hours to be with you. It's the least I can do."

Beth picked up two pies. "I'll put the desserts on the deck and give Eddie a hand. He's right. You've outdone yourself. I'll make a pot of tea for everyone."

I looked between them and hesitated. Eddie bobbed his head toward the sofa and winked. "Go. We've got this."

Lola meowed and sauntered into the room. I picked her up. "No snackies. You can have turkey for your dinner."

Herman floated past me. "Spoilsport."

Ignoring the snarky ghost, I sat down with Lola on my lap. "Gram, how was the turkey?"

She beamed. "Delicious, it was moist and flavorful. I couldn't have made any of the dishes better myself. Someone taught you well."

Everyone chuckled.

Mom said, "You don't get your kitchen skills from me."

"Dana, you don't cook?" Ethan asked.

"I don't cook holiday meals. That was Erma's claim to fame. My specialty is Italian. It's my favorite food, and when I toured Italy a few years back, I took several cooking classes and picked up a few tricks."

"Mom's being modest. She's an excellent cook and her homemade pasta begs to jump into her pots."

She blushed. "Claudia, stop."

Gram was always quick to offer a suggestion and said, "Maybe before we go back to Boston, you could cook for everyone."

"If I'm included," Fiona looked around the group, "I'll make focaccia."

"Of course, you're included…if everyone wants to eat my cooking." She gave Gram a stern look. "It's not like I have my special ingredients, though."

Ethan said, "You can use my kitchen. It's well stocked with herbs, spices, oils, and what I don't have, we can drive down to Portland and pick up. There are a couple of excellent authentic Italian markets."

"You're making it hard for me to refuse." Mom's cheeks flushed pink.

Was she flirting with Ethan? Was he flirting with her? Where was Beth when I needed her to witness this?

"Ethan, let me think about what I could make, and we can talk tomorrow. Erma and I aren't leaving until Tuesday or Wednesday."

He beamed. "After we close the knitting shop tomorrow, we can swing by my house, and I'll show you my kitchen." Clearing his throat, he glanced at the floor, "Of course you should stop by the store first. I'm sure Beth would love to show you and Erma around."

"Did I hear my name?" Beth asked as she and Eddie came in. Finally.

"Your dad invited Mom and Gram to visit your store, and he's trying to talk Mom into cooking us an Italian feast while she's here. In *his* kitchen." I felt I needed to add that so that she'd get the idea that something was simmering in my living room.

Fiona grinned. "I'm making bread."

Beth nodded. "That's a given, Fiona. Your bread-baking skills are incomparable. Sounds like we have a dinner party at Dad's. Sunday?"

Eddie said, "I'm free and hungry."

I twisted in my seat, looking up at him, and I arched one eyebrow. "After three slices of pie?"

He chuckled. "Well, I'll be hungry by Sunday."

I shook my head. "You're incorrigible."

Ethan leaned back on the sofa and crossed his ankle over his opposite knee. "Then it's settled. Dinner at my house on Sunday. Shall we say five for appetizers with dinner to follow?"

Mom smiled. "Since everyone seems to want to eat Italian, sure. Why not?"

From the windowsill, Herman said, "Romance is in the air."

I coughed, and everyone turned. Eddie rushed around the back of the sofa and knelt beside me. "Are you okay?"

I croaked, "Yes."

Gram stifled a laugh, and she gave a saucy wink to Herman's ghost. "We'll be staying at Whistler's Inn starting tomorrow. The reviews state they have an excellent breakfast."

Grateful for the change in topic and moving the focus from Ethan and Mom, I said, "Brewed Bliss has a wonderful plated breakfast on Sundays. That's if you feel like going out."

Fiona stood. "I'm going to walk around the block before going home. Would anyone care to join me?"

I set Lola on the floor and stretched my arms over my head as I stood. "I'll go with you." I was overly stuffed, and after the scare Fiona had a few months ago, I didn't want her walking alone—even if it wasn't dark yet, I'd feel better.

"Claudia, you don't need to hover. I have no ill effects since the bonk on my head."

Eddie said, "I'll walk with you ladies. I could work off a slice of pie so I can enjoy a sandwich later." He winked at me as I smiled my thanks.

"Well, that does sound lovely, being escorted by a handsome young man and my lovely friend."

I crossed to the closet, gathering our coats. Herman murmured, "As I said, romance is in the air."

Choosing to ignore him, and my grandmother's probing gaze, I held out Fiona's coat. "Here you are."

As she zipped it up, she said, "Will you bring my dishes back when they're empty?"

"Of course. I fixed a plate of leftovers for you on the porch and slivers of each dessert."

"Claudia, you're very thoughtful." She shook Mom's hand. "Dana, you have a charming daughter. Erma, meeting you was a pleasure, and I hope you stop by the shop. I have several pieces of vintage jewelry that you might like."

Gram gave her a warm hug. "Thank you. I look forward to browsing."

Herman drifted behind us as Eddie, Fiona, and I left. He pressed against the door—I'm sure wishing he could accompany Fiona home.

"Would you mind if we walked around before going back to my place? The fresh air will—" her words ended, and a muffled cry escaped her lips.

I slipped my arm around her shoulders. "Fiona, what's wrong?"

She sniffed. "This was the first normal Thanksgiving without Herman. Last year, my emotions were raw as he had just passed away, but being in your home today, I felt he was with us in spirit. It may sound bizarre, but… I wasn't sure I could face the holidays without him. However, we don't have a choice, do we?" She patted my arm. "It brought us all together. Herman would have loved that. Life marches on."

Eddie said, "It does, and I'm sure wherever Herman was, he peeked in on us and was happy the important people in his life were together, sharing a meal in his home."

Nodding, she said, "You're right. He would have been so happy to know Ethan and Beth were with you, Claudia, and her family around the table."

"And you, too, Fiona. I know in my heart that you were important to Herman." I didn't say he loved her, but I was sure they had cared deeply for each other and missed their chance at happiness as a couple.

She patted my hand. "Thank you, Claudia. You always know just what to say to comfort me."

We walked up the alley, across Cade Street, and turned right at the entrance of Lillith Park. White lights draped the evergreen trees around the park, and the menorah and Christmas tree stood in the center. "Darn, we're going to have a late dinner on Sunday. We won't want to miss the lighting ceremony at four. Gram specifically asked to go."

"We can remind Ethan when we return to the apartment."

Fiona sighed. "Drakes Bay is lovely this time of year, and Claudia, this is your first holiday season with us. I hope your sales are strong."

We strolled to the other side of the park and exited near the pharmacy on Main Street. The stillness of the early evening wrapped around us. I slipped my arm through the crook of Fiona's. "I discovered Herman sold gift cards for ready-to-wear items, but I'm going to offer them on anything in the store, including wedding dresses. What do you think?"

She beamed. "It's an excellent idea, especially considering how expensive a gown can be. Gift cards are always appreciated."

Knit or Purl was on the opposite side of the street. Beth had draped twinkle lights across her shop's front and her second-floor apartment windows, and a knitted wreath adorned her front door. It seemed many of the shop owners had decorated earlier in the day, and I was woefully behind.

"Eddie, after you get out of work tomorrow, would you

hold the attic ladder for me? I want to see what Herman had for holiday decorations."

Fiona said, "They won't all be in the attic. He stored some in the basement utility room. Either location, look for bright red totes."

I smiled. "Good to know."

A couple sat on suitcases as we approached the inn's front entrance. The man lifted his hand and smiled. "Happy Thanksgiving."

"Happy Thanksgiving," we said in unison.

Noticing that the inn's entrance was dimly lit, I asked, "Were you trying to check in?"

The man nodded. "Yes, but we're early. The innkeeper, Oliver Jones, texted and said they were running late and would be here by six."

I wondered why they weren't waiting in their car—not that it was any of my business.

Eddie glanced at his watch. "They should be along any minute. But if you're cold, you can wait in the lobby at the police station."

The woman shook her head and gave the man a sharp look.

He said, "Thank you. We're fine. Besides, we have friends checking in tonight. They'd worry if we weren't here when they arrived."

I said, "If you'd like, I could call Mariah Jones just to make sure they're on the way."

As I spoke, a Jeep with the inn's logo on the driver's side pulled up to the sidewalk. Oliver rolled the window down. "Hello. Are you the McGinty's?"

"No. I'm Clark Kline and my wife, Ava. Andi and Shawn McGinty, Pixie Bellamore, and Hugo West should arrive within the hour."

"Wonderful. I'll go around back and park. The front door will be open momentarily."

Mariah got out and walked in front of the Jeep. She waved at us, "Happy Thanksgiving, neighbors. Did your family arrive, Claudia?"

"They did, thanks. And they'll be checking in tomorrow."

"If they want to check in tonight, their rooms are ready."

"I'll let them know, but I'm looking forward to Mom and Gram staying with me."

With a wide smile, she said, "If you change your mind, send me a text, and I'll make sure to be at the front desk to greet them."

"I appreciate that. Have a good night." I nodded to the Kleins. "Enjoy your visit to Drakes Bay."

Mrs. Kline said, "I'm sure we will."

Fiona, Eddie, and I continued our walk past the front of Fiona's store and around the side. Like my apartment, she had an outside staircase leading to a deck with a similar view of the Atlantic.

"Thank you for the stroll and for a lovely holiday." She kissed my cheek and hugged Eddie. "You don't need to see me to the door."

Eddie said, "We'll wait until you're inside."

She smiled. "Claudia, hang on to this one. He's a keeper."

My face froze. The older generation was intent on making us a couple, between Herman's one-liner and now Fiona's comment. Not that I *really* minded; it was a dream to date Eddie. So far, we'd gone places as *just friends.*

She gave Eddie a pointed look. "Claudia's something special."

His eyes locked on mine. "Except when she's getting involved in a police matter. Then, she's something else."

Fiona laughed softly. "Be thankful she has an inquisitive mind. You never know when it might come in handy." She walked up the wooden stairs and waved when she reached the door.

Eddie and I stood silently before he said, "Care to stroll down the boardwalk before heading home?"

"We've got time." The sounds of car doors slamming and people's voices drifted to us. I said, "Sounds like the additional guests have arrived early."

He glanced in the direction of the inn. "So it seems. I thought the inn was closed for the day; that's why your family was staying the night with you."

"Oliver and Mariah must have made special considerations. Renting five additional rooms for tonight would help the bottom line. Yesterday, they decided to close since they were completely vacant until Saturday when they'd be fully booked."

"Huh, that seems odd with people traveling for the holiday weekend. When did Dana and Erma decide to move to the inn?"

I shrugged. "Today I guess." We came to the edge of the wooden planks. It was low tide and seaweed littered the beach. A deep, contented sigh escaped my lips. "I'll never get bored with this view or the salty tang in the air."

"Now, if you had an accent, you'd be mistaken for a Mainer." He shoulder-bumped me.

I looked at him. "This is the first time I've felt at home anywhere."

His eyes grew serious. "Despite the uptick in crime since you arrived? It used to be very safe to live here."

"It still is. A few bad actors can't change that."

He took my chilled hand. "I'm glad you moved here. Life has been a lot more interesting since you arrived."

My tummy flipped. I wasn't sure if I should say thank you or tell him that life was much more interesting for me, too. I opted for the less complicated answer, "Thanks. I think?"

He laughed. "Gigi, that was a compliment."

Smiling, I said, "We should get back to my place. I'm sure

you're hungry again and are ready to eat at least one sandwich and a slice of pie."

"You know me so well." He tugged me up the path. "What's your day look like tomorrow?"

"Busy. Fingers crossed, I sell a lot of ready-to-wear items and gift cards. But that's after I get Mom and Gram checked into the inn."

4

———————

The sun streamed through the living room windows and Lola stretched across the back of the sofa soaking up the warmth.

Herman lounged on his usual window ledge.

"Good morning." I rubbed Lola's ears after I rolled over on the soft cushions. "I'm the first one awake."

"It's the sun." Herman drifted to the loveseat. "What time is Erma going to the inn?"

"After breakfast. Why?"

"I was hoping to chat with her. It'd be nice to talk to someone my age for a change; it's been over a year since I've had a conversation with anyone but you."

"Herman, I'm sorry if I bore you." I swung my legs over the side. Lola hopped in my lap, purring.

"No, Claudia, it's not that. When I realized Erma could see and hear me, it felt like a light switch clicked on."

"Just because Gram and Mom are staying at the hotel for a few nights doesn't mean she won't come over here. Didn't you hear her say last night that she wants to help in the shop while she's here?" *Would my words comfort my uncle's ghost?*

He hung his head. "I get lonely. Not that it's your fault.

Before I died, I had friends and an active social life. Now, I'm stuck in this building like a prisoner, drifting between the attic and basement. Which reminds me—you need to have Beau Tinker check the attic before winter. I think there's a small leak around the window."

"Wait. How am I supposed to know about the leak? I can't get up there by myself."

"Eddie's coming over later to help with the decorations. Make sure you walk over to the window and notice the windowsill, it's stained dark. It might even be damp."

"Good idea. Thanks for the tip. And Herman, have you tried going beyond the walls? Even just on the deck?"

"Well, no. I figured, being a ghost and all, I was behind this veil when I died and didn't go to, like, the afterlife."

I smiled at him. "It's time to try." I stood, holding Lola, and crossed the room. Turning to Herman, I said, "Are you coming?" *Maybe there was something in that book I picked up,* Help Your Friendly Ghost Cross Over to the Afterlife. *I'd have to read another chapter soon.*

He floated next to me. "Are you sure I should try? What if something goes wrong and I disappear?"

"If you did, maybe that's how you cross over to the other side." My heart was heavy in my chest. "If you do, please know that this time together has been special for me, and I'll never forget you." I swallowed the unexpected lump that rose in my throat.

He drifted to the glass door. "I'm scared."

The tremor in his ghostly voice gave that away. "If you're not ready, don't do it."

"Claudia?"

I twirled around, "Gram. You're up early." She wore a thick bathrobe tied securely around her waist and pink fuzzy slippers

"What are you and Herman doing?"

He smiled his translucent grin. "Erma, I've decided to see

if I can venture outside. But we were discussing the possibility it's the portal to the great beyond, and I'm hesitating."

"Herman, it's been over a year since you died. Now that I've seen you and had the opportunity to tell you how much your support of Claudia has meant to me, you're ready if it's your time."

He leaned close to Lola. "My sweet baby girl, take care of Claudia for me." His hand almost rested on my arm. "You're going to do great things. Be brave and give yourself a chance to fall for Eddie. He's a good one." He moved in front of Erma and gave her a courtly bow. "I'm happy I got to see you again. You are a rare jewel, and I'm fortunate my brother had the good sense to marry you when he did so that you were part of our lives."

Placing my hand on the doorknob, I asked, "Herman, should I open the door, or do you want to try to float through it?"

"Open the door, please. Less resistance."

With a chuckle, I smiled, "Not that any wall inside has slowed you down." I held the door wide and cradled Lola in my arms. It wouldn't be good if she took off and I chased her down the stairs in my PJs and bare feet.

He gave me a worried look. "Can I have a countdown?"

"All right, on the count of three. One, two, two and a half," I paused to make sure he was prepared to make the next move.

He nodded.

"Three."

He floated through the open doorway and stopped at the edge of the deck, gazing at the ocean.

We followed him outside.

"Herman, you're still here."

He twirled around and grinned. "I am. Look at me on the deck." He zipped inside. "Can we try it with the door closed?"

I hurried in and closed the door with Gram near the railing.

He said, "Ready," and flew through the glass to the other side.

When I joined them, he was zipping around the deck. "I'm free. Free!"

"Can you go beyond the stairs?" Gram asked.

He floated over the edge, which caused my stomach to pitch, and drifted back to me. "Let's try the stairs," he said.

I waved a hand down my clothes. "I'm not dressed to be strolling down Cade Street. It would be better if we tried your little experiment another time."

"If you insist on waiting, I'll be patient." He raced from one side of the deck to the other. "This is amazing, the freedom of being outside. Who would have thought how happy this would make me? Erma, can you believe it?"

She nodded. "You didn't cross over."

His face fell. "I wonder why?"

"I'm going in to feed Lola and start coffee. Herman, are you coming?"

"Erma, would you stay out here with me for a bit so we can chat? You don't want Dana to overhear you having a conversation with yourself."

Gram laughed. "That wouldn't be easy to explain." She waved me away. "If your mother gets up before I come in, just tell her I'm soaking in the salt air. It's good for my complexion."

I dropped a kiss on her lined cheek. "You got it." After I closed the door, I watched her sit down, and Herman perched on the railing. If a ghost could look happy, mine was thrilled.

*T*he nip in the breeze added a festive air as Mom, Gram, and I walked through the alley to the front door of Whistlers Inn.

Mariah was behind the narrow wood counter on the phone when we entered. She waved and held up a finger to indicate she'd be another minute. I set their tote bags down.

Mom wandered around the spacious lobby and coffee nook. "Look at this portrait of a man." She leaned closer and said, "Thomas Pennington. He has kind eyes. I wonder who he was?"

Since I had no idea, I pointed to the next room. "Mom, the dining area is through the arch and to the right. It has a lovely view of the ocean."

Gram sat in a chair after pouring herself a cup of coffee. I'd kept a close eye on her since she and Herman talked. Even though she admitted she could see ghosts like me, she had never talked with one until Herman. It had to have been unnerving. I know it had taken me a bit to adjust to talking with him.

She noticed me looking and gave me a guarded smile. Maybe once Mom was in her room, we could talk privately for a moment.

"I'm sorry you had to wait," Mariah's voice was perky. "Mrs. Grant and Mrs. Grant. I have reserved two lovely adjoining rooms overlooking the ocean for you."

Mom handed her a credit card. "This is for both rooms."

"Give me a moment." She took the card and wrote down some information before placing two old-fashioned keys on the counter.

Feet clomping on the staircase drew my attention. The couple from last night and two more couples reached the bottom.

Mariah smiled. "Good morning, everyone. Breakfast is around the corner. Help yourselves. There's an urn of fresh coffee and dispensers for hot water if you fancy tea."

Mr. Kline said, "Thanks."

His wife said to the others, "Go on in. I want a word with Mariah." She waited until they were out of hearing range before turning to the innkeeper. "Thank you again for allowing us to check in on the holiday. When Andi insisted we leave the other gathering early, I wasn't sure if you would accommodate us." Her lips thinned, "But the world revolves around her, and she was confident you'd welcome us."

Mariah smiled at Mrs. Klein. "It's fine. I was glad you called and happy to welcome you to Drakes Bay."

"The others won't see it as though you went out of your way, but I do." She gave me a curt nod as she left the room.

"That was very nice, Mariah. I know you offered for Mom and Gram to come over last night but renting four rooms for an extra night was a bonus."

She frowned. "Five rooms, and they're a bit…" she looked at the dining room door before she continued, "demanding."

"Oh, I just assumed it was three couples."

"No, a brother and sister, a pair of cousins, and one couple, I think. From what they said, they all went to school together except for Ava Kline. That's the girl who was just here. She married into the group, and the other girl, Pixie Bellamore, she's friends with Ava from before the wedding. At least that's what I overheard when Andi was talking with her brother."

Mom said, "Ava seems pleasant."

"Wait until you bump into the others. They are the full range of customers if you get my meaning." Mariah slid a paper across the counter to Mom. "Sign here, please, and I'll show you to your rooms."

I picked up my grandmother's bag. "Ready to get settled in, Gram?"

She brushed her hand down the front of her new pleated skirt, which she paired today with a cream-colored silk blouse and a suede blazer. It matched the burgundy plaid perfectly. "After I've unpacked, I'll come to your shop to help."

Mom said, "Erma, I'm sure Claudia doesn't need us

hanging around. Besides, I told Ethan we'd stop by Beth's store."

"You can do both." I smiled, hoping to keep everyone happy, but to see Mom's cheeks flush when she mentioned Ethan tickled me.

As we walked toward the stairs, a girl hurried from the dining room, running straight into my grandmother, spilling a glass of orange juice down her blouse and skirt.

"Oh, no," Gram cried, "Look at my new skirt."

"Jeez, I'm sorry. I'll pay to have your outfit dry cleaned." The petite girl looked at my grandmother. "I'm Andi McGinty, staying in room four." She glanced at Mariah. "Is there a dry cleaner in town?" Her breath came in fast and shallow gasps.

"No need for that. The skirt can be hand washed," I said. "Gram, your blazer seems to have been missed."

The young woman pressed her hand to her heart. "Then, I'll wash your skirt if Mariah gives me access to her laundry room."

"There's no need. I'll take care of it," I said.

Mariah interjected. "That's not necessary, Claudia. I can rinse it out and toss it in the dryer."

I shook my head. "It has to dry flat."

"I have a table to dry my sweaters. Really, I can take care of this for her."

Gram's gaze slipped from me to Mariah and then to Andi. "It seems everyone wants to help. Andi, thank you for the offer. We'll manage to get it cleaned. Just try to be more careful when rushing around with a glass of juice."

Her pale skin brightened as she patted the front of her red sweater. "Well, I'm dry and if you're all set, I'm going to run up to my room. I need to get my shoulder bag and meet the guys before we leave to explore the town. It has my medicine and gum. See ya." Dashing up the stairs, she stumbled at the top. Holding onto the banister for support, she paused for a moment, leaning against the wall and then disappeared around the corner.

"Mrs. Grant?" Mariah said.

Mom and Grandma both looked at her.

With a laugh, Mom said, "How about you call us Dana and Erma? It will be easier for everyone."

"Okay, Erma. If you bring your skirt down, I'll have it cleaned for you by the end of the day."

"I'll do that." Gram and I climbed the stairs. "It's too bad, though. I wanted to show off my beautiful outfit so that I was living advertisement for you, my darling girl."

"The good news, Gram, is that I have plenty of skirts to match your outfit. You can choose whatever you'd like and be a walking billboard."

With a twinkle in her eye, she patted my arm. "The next skirt I'm buying."

*G*randma flipped over the OPEN sign to CLOSED. She exhaled. "Is that what a normal day is like in your shop?"

I laughed. "Not ever. I sold gift cards, every knitted item Beth had in the shop, and a good portion of my ready-to-wear line. Tonight, I'll restock and see if Beth has anything on the shelf at her store that she can put back into inventory."

Herman drifted into the main salon. "Claudia, the shop has never done this kind of business the day after Thanksgiving. You've got the Midas touch."

Since Mom was upstairs, I was free to talk with my ghost. "That's sweet, Herman, but I'm worried that I'll disappoint more customers if I don't have enough inventory."

"Nonsense. Leave them wanting more, and maybe you'll sell more gift cards. You can also remind customers they're valid for spring dresses, too."

"Good point."

"Erma, you're quite the dynamo in sales. You should hang around the shop tomorrow. It's Small Business Saturday."

"I think I will. But for today, I'm exhausted. A hot bath, a nice plate of leftovers, and a glass of wine with a slice of pie in the lounge sounds like heaven. If Mariah doesn't mind."

"All that can be arranged, Gram. I'll walk you back to the inn and let Mom know the plan."

"You should call Beth to see if she and Ethan care to join us. I'm sure Dana would like to visit with him—I mean, *them*."

I winked at her. "You're a hopeful romantic. I need to talk to Beth, anyway." I got our coats off the hook in the back and said, "Herman, I'll be back shortly. Keep your eye on things."

"Isn't Eddie coming over later?"

"Yes, I won't be gone long. For now, I'll get Gram settled and be back to pack up the leftovers."

G ram and I walked to the corner, and I glanced toward the police station. "Eddie said he'd stop by to help me get the decorations down."

She pulled the collar of her coat closer to her neck. "Maybe he should join us for leftovers."

In the growing dusk, we strolled to the inn's front entrance. As I pushed the door open, a scream pierced the serenity.

Rushing inside, I scanned the room. "Gram, wait here."

"HELP!"

The scream came from the back of the building. I ran through the door into a large kitchen and paused.

"HURRY!"

Gram was one step behind me.

A door stood open, and I could see a washer and dryer. "Mariah?"

"Yes, come quick."

I rushed in and skidded to a stop. Cradled in her arms was Andi McGinty, the guest from this morning. My grandmother's pleated skirt wrapped around her neck like a scarf, but that wasn't what held me back. Her lips were swollen and red and she didn't look like she was breathing.

"Gram, call 9-1-1 and wait for the police out front."

She hurried from the room.

"Claudia, I found her like this about a half hour ago, and she's cold."

Mariah's eyes were wide, skin flushed, and her breathing was coming rapidly, as she clung to Andi's lifeless form. "Mariah, place her body on the floor and slide away."

Based on the way Andi's lips and face were distorted, she'd either eaten something she's allergic to or she'd been poisoned.

5

———

Mariah clung to my hand as my grandmother hovered in the doorway. Gram said, "The police should be here soon."

I nodded to show that I heard her. "Mariah, do you have any idea what happened?"

She shook her head. Stumbling back a few steps her face drenched in horror. "I wasn't told about allergies. I would have made sure there was nothing in the building she could have come in contact with."

Continuing to hold her trembling hand, I slipped my other arm around her rigid body. "We should go to the lobby." Distracting her so she wasn't staring at the body was the first thing I needed to do. "Where's Oliver?"

With a shrug, a cry slipped from her lips, and she buried her face in my shoulder. "They're going to think I killed her."

"No one will blame you. That's not something you need to worry about. The police are good at their jobs, and they'll find the person responsible." I pushed from my memory that when I moved to town, I had been a primary suspect in a murder, and when Fiona had been attacked, the new cop in town, Rhonda Perkins, would have been happy to pin that crime on me, too. It stuck in her craw that I was instrumental in solving both crimes. I looked around the tidy room; nothing seemed out of place. "Gram, take my phone and snap pictures of every wall, surface, and the floor." I withdrew the device from my pocket and handed it to her.

"Right." She entered my password as I said it and took pictures while I guided Mariah from the room.

Escorting her down the hall, I steered her to an over-stuffed chair and knelt beside her for a few moments. "My grandmother will stay with you while I talk with the police." When she didn't respond, I pulled a chair over for Gram. "I'll be back as soon as I can."

Mariah rubbed her breastbone as she took shaky breaths.

Gram said, "Do what you need to do. But Claudia, be extra careful. We don't know if an unsavory sort is lingering in the shadows."

I wiped my clammy hand down my pant leg. "I will." My heart constricted as I remembered the vibrant young woman from this morning; she was full of life.

The door to the inn opened. Eddie strode in with Rhonda behind him.

"Claudia, what's happened?" His face was devoid of emotion, but his eyes slid from my toes to my eyes. "Are you hurt?"

"No." I wrapped my arms around my midsection, doing my best not to shiver. "My grandmother and I came to the inn. When we walked in, we heard Mariah scream for help. We found her in the laundry room off the kitchen. She was on the floor cradling one of the guests, Andi McGinty, in her arms. I think she ingested something that either caused an allergic reaction, or she was poisoned."

"What makes you an expert?" Rhonda glared at me.

"The bloating of her face caused her lips to swell and take on a purplish-red color. Oh, and not to be derailed from the physical details, she has a pleated skirt around her neck like a scarf."

"A skirt? Are you sure she wasn't strangled?" Eddie asked.

I paused. "No, it's artfully arranged, not tight. It's possible it was loosened afterward, but my guess is no."

"Claudia, leave the investigation and probabilities to the authorities." Rhonda stepped around me and glanced over her shoulder. "I'll meet you in the back when you're done questioning the witness."

At least she hadn't said suspect. "Eddie, I didn't touch anything, but Mariah may have." Bobbing my head toward the lobby, I lowered my voice. "My grandmother stayed with Mariah. Understandably, she's in shock."

"You didn't see or hear anything unusual when you entered the building, and no one was running away?"

"We came down the street. I wanted to see the decorations and get some fresh air. It was super busy at the shop today."

He nodded and waited.

"This morning, when I brought Mom and Gram to check in, Andi, the dead girl, spilled orange juice on Gram's skirt. Mariah said she'd launder it."

"How did Erma come into contact with the victim?"

"Andi rushed around a corner to go to her room when they collided. She said she had to get her medicine—I assumed she needed to take it with food."

"Was she rude to Erma?"

"Not at all. She offered to pay for dry cleaning or launder it herself, but I told her it was washable, and Mariah volunteered to take care of it."

"Do you think it was just an accident? Bad timing on her part?"

I didn't have to think about his question. "Definitely bad timing."

"All right. I'd like to talk with Mariah before I review the crime scene."

"Is the ambulance on the way?"

"Yes, and I have called in the state police crime scene team. With Amos no longer available," he coughed, "we need the state's support."

Amos Brand was wearing prison orange after using his position to shake down business owners and trying to pin a murder on me to protect his girlfriend. "I'm sure the state police will be an asset." Is that what I should have said, or should I have avoided the topic altogether? It was tough to know what to say in these situations. "It's good to know you have support." I walked beside him as we entered the main lobby. Mariah was pale, her mouth gaped open, and she clung to Gram.

She stood when she saw us. "Eddie, I didn't kill that poor girl."

He gestured for her to sit. "Mariah, no one said that you did. However, I need to ask you some questions. Are you up for that?"

"Anything you need," she folded her hands on her lap. "I wish Oliver was here."

Eddie asked, "Where is he? I'll call him for you."

"I'm not sure. I went to Polly's Pantry for a few things, and when I returned, the Jeep was gone, and he didn't leave a note."

"Is that out of character for him?"

She bit her lower lip. "Yes. Do you think something could have happened to him, too? If there's a killer on the loose—" Looking from Eddie to me, she teared up, "Can I call him?"

"Do you have your cell?"

"It's on the desk." She leaned forward and I placed a hand on her shoulder.

"I'll get it for you." Crossing the room, I stood behind the counter scanning the area for her cell phone when I noticed powdered residue on the shelf. "Eddie, you should see this."

"Did you find something?"

I tipped my head from side to side. "You can be the judge of that."

He pressed his hand on mine. "Don't touch anything and leave the cell where it is. The staties need to see this."

"You're the boss." I went back to Mariah and handed her my cell. "Use mine to call Oliver."

She glanced at me; fear lingered in her eyes. "What's wrong?"

"There may be evidence under the counter. Eddie wants that area processed."

Her eyes widened. "Oh-Em-Gee. I'm going to jail."

Squatting down at her eye level, I took her hand. "Mariah, if it's evidence, it doesn't mean you had anything to do with it. Think logically; you have an entire building at your disposal. If you had wanted to poison the woman, you wouldn't have done anything that could be traced back to you."

Taking a stuttered breath, she bobbed her head. "Right. This is overwhelming."

"Will you give me your husband's cell number?"

Rattling off the numbers, I dialed and handed her the phone. The corners of her lips dipped. "Ollie, I need you to call me immediately or better still get back to the inn. There's been a death."

She disconnected and handed me the phone. "That will get him to call me back."

Personally, I thought it was a bit harsh, but he wasn't my husband, and she knew best how to get his attention. Three police officers entered the lobby and scanned the room.

One nodded at Eddie, and he walked over to the counter. "Trooper Stanton, MSP."

"Jacobs. Thanks for coming."

"What can you tell us?" The officer's voice was devoid of inflection. The two remaining officers waited.

"A young woman, age unknown, was discovered in the laundry room unresponsive, presumed to be deceased. Based on a bystander's observation, it could be from an allergic reaction or poison, and she had a skirt tied around her neck. The innkeeper, Mariah Jones, discovered her…"

I said, "Thirty minutes ago, plus the time it took for the police to arrive."

Eddie said, "Forty minutes, give or take."

The officer gave me a cursory look. "And the woman was dead when she was discovered?"

Nodding, I said, "Yes, she wasn't breathing and was cold."

Mariah said. "That equals dead."

I was surprised at the anger-laced words. It seemed the shock had worn off.

Trooper Stanton came over to Mariah. "You are?"

"Mariah Jones, my husband Oliver and I own Whistlers Inn. Andi McGinty checked in last night with her brother and four friends."

"Do you know where these people are now?"

She shook her head. "I had been in the basement storage room getting the holiday decorations. This was after I laundered Mrs. Grant's skirt and laid it out to dry. This morning, Andi spilled juice on it."

"What happened next?"

Gesturing toward the plastic totes on the opposite side of the lobby, she said, "I brought up the bins, and before I started decorating, I ran across the street to the market to get a few things for dinner."

"Did you know the victim was in the building?"

"I saw the group leave a few minutes before lunch. They were going out shopping and for a walk on the beach. I heard one of the guys say, "You need to take a chill pill. Things will get better soon."

The trooper remained expressionless. "Those were the exact words?"

She nodded. "But I don't know who said it or who they said it to. Their backs were to me as they walked out the front door."

"You're sure it was a man?"

Her face screwed up as she seemed to be replaying the conversation in her head. "Ya know, now that I think of it, a woman made the statement."

He nodded. "Good."

Eddie said, "Before you arrived, we discovered a white powdery substance behind the counter."

Trooper Stanton looked at the other officers. He said, "One to the laundry room, the other start behind the counter."

They split off in two directions. Eddie called after the one striding down the hall to where the body was, "Officer Perkins is in there."

I gave him a quizzical glance. Why hadn't Rhonda returned? Could she have found something important? But I didn't ask the questions.

Eddie lifted a shoulder and said nothing.

The front door banged open, and Oliver ran in, sliding over the polished wood floor to a stop. "Mariah, what happened? Are you okay? I saw the police cars outside and…" He took a deep breath and looked around the room. "Eddie, what's happened?"

"Mariah found one of your guests who has died under suspicious circumstances. When Claudia and Erma arrived, they called the police."

That was a succinct way of relaying the facts.

The color drained from his face, and he stumbled back, grabbing the door casing for support. "Who?"

"Andi McGinty."

"Which one was she?"

"Room four."

"Her? She was the nicest of the lot."

I perked up. What did Oliver mean?

Eddie asked, "Would you elaborate on that statement?"

Oliver said, "The married couple, the Klines, seem to be the leaders of the bunch. Whatever they say, the others agree to. Andi's brother, Shawn, is overprotective of his sister, and the other two are rude. All in all, four of the six act like the world owes them a favor."

Trooper Stanton asked, "Did you overhear anyone arguing with the victim?"

"No." He took Mariah's hand. "Did you?"

"I didn't hear anyone fighting, but they disagreed about where they were going for dinner tonight. Andi didn't want to have to travel far—she mentioned her stomach wasn't feeling well and didn't want to have motion sickness on top of it."

"You don't expect them back anytime soon?" the trooper asked.

"It's hard to say, but wouldn't they return since Andi hadn't? They must have known she was coming back to the inn."

"Mr. Jones, would you come with me please?" The officer pointed to the kitchen door. Oliver kissed Mariah's cheek and left the room.

Mariah made an excellent point. I looked at my grandmother, who remained quiet during the questioning. She shrugged.

"I provided them with a list of good restaurants in the area, but they preferred an excellent seafood place with a relaxed atmosphere. Pixie mentioned they wanted a dining experience as close to eating on a pier as possible."

Stanton never broke his gaze with her. "Did you give them a suggestion?"

"The only place like that that's open year around and

close enough is the Clam Shack in Pembroke Cove out on Route One."

He nodded. "I know the place, but you're right. They should come back to the inn unless they had a falling out and went without her."

Rhonda came into the room. "Officer Jacobs. A moment?"

He walked past me, but I couldn't catch his eye. I casually moved through the room, lingering near the doorway. Rhonda had her back to me, and Eddie didn't acknowledge me. I turned so that my back was to them, as if I were studying the painting over the fireplace.

"Trooper Anson wanted you to know he's detected a strong spicy odor on the victim." She nodded to Stanton. "If you can let the others know, he'd appreciate it."

"She wasn't strangled?"

Rhonda shook her head. "Claudia was correct, it was poison. But don't tell her I said that. She'll get a big head and think she can work the case from the sidelines with your cousin, Beth." She held up her hand. "Before you deny it, I know what she and Beth did on the button and burglary case and the attack on Fiona. It was beginners' luck."

His voice was stern when he said, "That was the second time she helped the police."

"Interfered. Jacobs, that was the last time she will meddle in one of my cases."

"Perkins, you forget I'm the senior officer in the department and I can use resources that I deem appropriate."

Ice cracked from her next words. "If you want to put her in danger, then go ahead. Your girlfriend's neck won't be on my conscience." She stomped away.

I froze in place. How could I make it seem like I hadn't overheard the part about me being Eddie's girlfriend? We hadn't dated; We had just hung out with Beth and Luke at the fall festival in Pembroke Cove and had an occasional pizza night.

Eddie tapped my shoulder. "Did you get all that?"

"Spicy. Maybe she just brushed her teeth, and it was minty?"

His brow quirked, and a question lingered on his face. I chose to ignore the *girlfriend* comment and focus on the critical information—it was poison.

"It seems your initial impression was correct—but do me a favor and don't gloat to Officer Perkins; she's a little prickly where you're concerned."

"Ya think?" I smiled, trying to ease the awkwardness between us. He knew that I'd heard everything she'd said. But we weren't about to broach it. As far as I was concerned, I had to skirt any talk of me, him, or whatever might or might not be between us.

My grandmother's eyes darted to the hall leading to the front door, and I looked in the same direction.

A translucent form hovered a foot off the floor. "I feel funny."

Andi McGinty was a ghost.

6

———

$\mathscr{I}$ looked at Gram, and she winked. We both had heard Andi McGinty's ghost speak. Dang it. Somehow, I was going to have to get her alone and see what I could learn about why and how she was killed…and who did it. But first, based on her question, she had no idea she's a ghost. How do I explain that?

My gaze bounced to Gram and then to Eddie. I needed the ghost to follow me. So, Gram needed to distract him.

She coughed. "Eddie, dear. Would you be able to get me a glass of water?"

Mariah said, "I'll get it for you."

Patting the younger woman's arm, she nodded to Eddie. "I'm sure the nice police officer won't mind. Stay with me. You've had quite a shock." She coughed again for good measure.

Eddie said, "Certainly, Erma. Mariah, you should stay with her." He left the room, and I hurried over to the ghost. Her watery brown eyes locked onto mine.

"I know you." She tipped her head. "Do you know why I feel so odd?"

I glanced over my shoulder. "Gram, I'm going to step outside for a minute and get a bit of air."

"Go ahead, dear. We'll be fine right here."

I whispered to the ghost, "Follow me."

"Where are we going?" She drifted behind me and out the door as I opened it.

Not seeing anyone I said, "Andi, come with me."

"Don't I need a coat?"

"Sadly, no." I stepped away from the inn into a garden where I could speak freely. I was glad that I wore my jacket to shield against the brisk ocean breeze.

Looking at her feet, she said, "At least I have boots on." Then she shrieked. "My feet aren't touching the ground. How's that possible?"

"Andi, there's no easy way to tell you this news, but when my grandmother and I returned to the inn, we found Mariah cradling your body in her arms. You died."

She narrowed her eyes and clenched her fists at her sides. "What do you mean? If I'm dead, how am I talking to you?"

I didn't need a ticked-off ghost on my hands. The only time I've talked to them—my uncle and a ghost in an antique jeweler's shop in Portland—the exchanges were pleasant. I had never talked to a recently departed version.

"Andi, I have a unique gift; I can talk to ghosts." I looked at how far we were from the inn. It was easily thirty feet from the door. How was it that Andi could be out here when Herman had just stepped onto the deck? Was it possible, due to her recent demise, her ghost had different abilities? I'd have to look this up in the book I was reading.

"I'm a ghost? Well, this stinks. How did I die?" She tried to snap her fingers, but her thumb morphed into her middle finger. With a shake of her body and slumped shoulders. "Was there water on the floor causing me to slip and crack my head open? Can I sue?"

"No. There was no water, and there's no reason to sue. You were," I gulped, "poisoned."

"What?" Her form shot up ten feet into the air, like a toy rocket propelled by a rubber band, and then back down. Her voice quivered. "Poisoned?"

"Yes. My grandmother's pleated skirt was draped around your neck like a scarf. What do you remember? Anything at all?"

She drifted a few feet away from me and then back, almost as if pacing. "It's a blank."

"What's the last thing you *do* remember?"

Closing her eyes, she said, "The juice drenching your grandmother's skirt. I went upstairs. I had a migraine starting, and I wanted to nip it before it got worse."

"That was seven hours ago."

"Fine, poke at me, and I'll haunt you forever." She twirled around leaving her back to face me.

I couldn't help but giggle. "I already live with a ghost, my uncle. And with some luck, you should cross over once we solve your death." I didn't want to say murder; that would upset her.

"And leave my brother?" She crossed her arms over her chest. "I don't think I'm going anywhere."

"Sadly, if you don't cross over, you'll never check out of the inn."

"You mean I'll be stuck here forever?"

"Seems so." I waited for that to sink in. Were all ghosts this lucid right after dying? I'd have to ask Herman about his experience. "Let's get back to today."

Her lips formed a pout. "Fine. After breakfast and meds, we went out shopping. There's the charming second-hand shop next door, and then we had a late lunch at Brewed Bliss. After that, we strolled on the beach, trying to decide where we'd go for dinner. I wanted to get an ice cream from the place up the street."

"Scoop-a-licious?"

"Right, and then a cruise through the park. I guess there's going to be a lighting ceremony soon." Her face fell. "I'll miss the holidays."

"After you went to Lillith Park, you returned to the inn alone?"

"I wanted to check on Mrs. Grant's skirt. If the orange juice hadn't washed out, I planned on replacing it from your shop."

She grabbed for my hand, but hers slipped right through. Would I ever get used to that topsy-turvy feeling when a ghost tried to touch me?

"What is it?"

"The last moment I remember was tossing my coat and handbag on the bench at the base of the stairs. The rest is," she squeezed her eyes shut, "blank."

Air escaped my lungs in a *whoosh*. Andi couldn't tell me who killed her. "Did you come back to the inn alone?"

"Claudia?" Eddie stood in the door. "What are you doing outside?"

I spun around and gave him a wave. "I needed some fresh air and to think."

A quizzical look quirked his brow. "Were you talking to yourself?"

I crossed my fingers behind my back. "Yup, just sorting out everything that happened. I'll be right in?" I shouldn't have phrased that as a question; my voice just jumped an octave. Fibbing to Eddie wasn't the right thing to do, but he'd never believe me if I said I was talking to the victim's ghost.

Making it a statement I said, "I'll be right in."

He seemed to waver, almost as if he were going to stay, but then he turned his head. "I gotta go," and closed the door.

There was a tiny lead. Andi's coat and purse should be on the bench. "Are you ready to go inside?"

Her ghost nodded. "You can't talk to me in there, can you?"

My heart ached for her. I understood from living with Herman the isolation a ghost could feel. "I can't, but if we need to talk, we can come outside again. Is that all right?"

"It'll have to be." She drifted to the inn's main entrance. "You're Claudia?"

"I am."

"At least I have one person to talk with." Her voice held a depth of sadness I hadn't heard with Herman. That was probably because he had been a ghost for several months before I moved to town.

"My grandmother, Mrs. Grant, has the same ability—so there are two of us."

"That's some consolation."

I opened the door, and she drifted to the bottom of the stairs, twirling in a three-sixty. "Claudia, my coat's gone. So's my bag."

"Maybe it's in your room?" I dropped my voice to a whisper because talking to myself was better than appearing to talk with ghosts.

The ghostly figure zipped up the staircase and vanished from view. I wanted to follow Andi, but doing so would seem suspicious.

Eddie crossed the room. "Is everything all right?"

"If Andi was out with her friends and came back to the inn for an unknown reason, where's her coat?"

He looked around. "Wasn't she wearing it?"

"No. When I saw Andi this morning, she had on a red cable turtleneck sweater and dark jeans."

"Good to know. I'll check the laundry room to see if her coat's in there." He walked away and, over his shoulder, said, "Wait here."

"Too bad, I had a good idea," I called after him, not trying to be sassy since I was sure it wasn't there.

Andi hovered at the base of the stairs. "Claudia, psst."

Gram placed herself between Mariah and me so that I could hear what Andi had discovered. I sidestepped to where the ghost hovered.

"What did you find out?"

"My room is a disaster. I'm super tidy—like everything has a place," her ghostly apparition frowned, "well, had a place, and clothes are everywhere; my makeup is on the floor."

"Are you saying your room's been ransacked?"

She nodded.

"Did you find your bag and coat?"

"No." She drifted closer to me. "If I was poisoned, how did it happen?"

"That's a good question and what you've told me is an important clue." I scanned the room for coffee cups, glasses, or even a water bottle. Every surface was devoid of anything that could have contained a beverage.

Eddie came in and stared at me. "No coat or bag. I'm going to check her room."

"Can I come if I stay in the hall?"

He hesitated. "Not one toe in the room. Understood? This is an active investigation."

"Got it."

Taking the stairs two at a time, he asked, "Do you know her room number?"

"Four. But you'll need a key."

He held up a single skeleton key. "I have a master."

We came around the corner; I stopped short. "The door's ajar."

"Stay back." Easing it open, he took a tentative step inside.

Craning my neck for a better view, sure enough, Andi's room looked like it had been turned upside down and shaken.

"She wasn't tidy."

"I've lived with women who aren't neat; this room has been searched." I stood in the open door and shivered. When Eddie went into the adjoining bath, I hastily took as many pictures as possible before he returned.

Stepping over a pile of cosmetics, a box of Band-Aids, and two packs of gum, he knelt in front of a prescription bottle.

"This morning, when she bumped into my grandmother, Andi mentioned she was going to her room to get medicine for an oncoming migraine." *Shoot she told me the migraine part after she died.*

"That's good to know." Standing, he crossed to the open window. "There's no screen, and the window's ajar. There might be enough room for someone to have left it partially open before jumping to the ground."

"Maybe Andi had the window open for fresh air and forgot to close it." The ghost pushed through me, and I softly groaned. Talk about queasy… "How could someone have left through the window and closed it at all?"

"Are you okay?" he asked.

"I'm fine, just hungry." I leaned over the threshold but didn't step over it. "Any chance I can have a picture of the window?"

Eddie said, "No. It's official police business, and you need to stay out of this investigation. Besides, I don't want Rhonda to have a reason to arrest you for interference."

My hand flew to cover my mouth. Stammering, I asked, "Sh-she wouldn't, would she?"

"Don't push her, and we won't find out." His face softened even if his tone didn't. "Gigi, please, don't get involved any more than you already are. Whoever killed Andi McGinty wasn't messing around. The poison had to have been strong enough to kill her quickly."

I withdrew my cell and tapped in how fast rat poison kills a human. "Rat poison is bitter to humans, so that wasn't used." I kept reading. "But cyanide is tasteless, and guess what?" I looked at Eddie. "It causes headaches, vertigo, and weakness. Maybe it was a longer-term trickle of poison and not a single dose."

He rubbed the back of his neck. "Stop spinning theories."

I gave him a side glance. "But your brain's gone into overdrive. I can tell by the wrinkle between your brows. I'm on to something. Admit it."

"Not gonna happen, Gigi. This time, I'm not sharing."

"Does this mean you won't reconsider taking a picture of the window for me?"

"What do you mean I was poisoned more than just once? Someone was methodically killing me?" Andi's ghostly form vibrated as her voice rose. It was a good thing Eddie couldn't see or hear her since he'd be at a loss as to how to handle it.

I needed to get the ghost away from here. Unlike Herman, she seemed volatile in this state. "Never mind about the pictures. Oddly, no one has returned to the inn looking for her. Surely, she said she wouldn't have been gone long."

The walkie-talkie clipped to his shoulder crackled.

Rhonda's voice cut like a razor. "Jacobs, the victim's brother and friends have arrived. Meet me in the lobby."

Tapping the switch, he glanced at me before saying, "On my way." He scanned the room again and, using the mic, said, "Send up an officer. I need room four sealed."

"Roger that."

He crossed the space and was less than a foot from me. "Are you a mind-reader?"

My voice held a hint of laughter as I told him the truth without telling him. "No, just a ghost whisperer."

"Right." He gestured for me to step back. "Ask our victim who killed her and how."

"If only it worked that way, Officer Jacobs."

Andi hovered close. "Does he believe you?"

Ignoring the ghost, I asked, "Can I be nearby when you tell the friends and family?"

With a heavy sigh, he said, "You'll be in the vicinity, so I can't stop you from eavesdropping unless I send you home. But you haven't given your full statement to the state police officers, yet…"

My eyes widened, "Don't you have jurisdiction?"

"I do, but they're assisting with the investigation, and Trooper Stanton might have a few questions for you and Erma." He pointed to the steps. "We must go. I'm needed downstairs."

Andi's ghost drifted next to me, silent as we descended the stairs. In the living room, a small group of five people stood. She said, "My brother is standing next to the fireplace. Hugo and Pixie are near the window, and Clark and Ava are about to sit on the sofa."

Rhonda and Trooper Stanton waited in the room. He glanced at us when Eddie entered. Hoping to appear uninterested, I sank onto the wooden riser that had a clear view of everyone. Andi hovered next to her brother.

"I'm Officer Jacobs." He gestured to Rhonda and the trooper. "Officer Perkins and Trooper Stanton of the Maine State Police. I'm sorry to tell you that a short while ago, Andi McGinty was discovered in the laundry room. Dead."

Clark snorted. "Did she put you up to this macabre game of Clue? It was her favorite when we were kids. Ms. McGinty, in the laundry room with a wrench?"

Pixie giggled. "Andi wouldn't be caught dead in a laundry room."

Ava clung to Clark's hand and grimaced. "Pixie, really?"

Clark glanced at Ava as color drained from his face.

Hugo and Pixie's voices faded from high spirts to somber as Eddie remained quiet.

Shawn stepped forward. Andi tried to stop him, but her

hand slid through his arm. "You can't be serious. My sister came back to check on that skirt."

Eddie said, "Mr. McGinty, this is not a game. I'm sorry for your loss."

He blanched. "Where's my sister? I want to see her now!"

Andi floated to me. "He can't see me, can he?"

I shook my head. "This is a tragedy."

7

———————

$\mathcal{R}$honda stepped between Eddie and Hugo, Pixie, and the Clarks. She gestured Shawn toward the hall. "Officer Jacobs will escort you, Mr. McGinty."

His head jerked as he straightened his shoulders. "How will she look?"

Andi said, "He's squeamish. This won't be pretty."

That was an understatement on so many levels. I stood and waited for Eddie and Shawn to leave the room.

He glared at Mariah as he crossed to the hallway that led to where Andi was lying. "What did you do?"

She jumped to her feet. "No one said anything about allergies, and I haven't fixed her anything since breakfast. If your sister ate or drank something that harmed her, it's not my fault. I don't have poison just lying around."

Shawn froze. "What's she talking about, poison? My sister's been poisoned? How? What kind of poison? She wouldn't willingly ingest something that could kill her. I demand answers now!"

"Mr. McGinty, we're examining every possible way your sister may have come in contact with a deadly substance."

"Since you're not wearing masks, it wasn't airborne."

That was an excellent observation, and I was impressed that he was thinking somewhat clearly.

"No, sir. We believe, based on the evidence, your sister ingested it."

I rubbed the center of my aching chest. I had never been near anyone who was about to face the death of their loved one under suspicious circumstances. Eddie was compassionate, and even Rhonda's sensitivity in staying with the others to give Shawn the privacy he deserved was commendable.

Shawn dropped his chin to his chest. "I'm ready."

I hung back. He needed privacy, and with the police around, this would be very difficult for him without me tagging along.

Mariah slumped in a chair and stared out the window, chewing on a fingernail. Andi drifted behind her brother.

"Gram, I'm going to call Beth and Mom to let them know we've been held up."

She nodded. I went outside and ensured the door shut before wandering around the side of the building to where I thought I'd have an excellent view of Andi's open bedroom window. The screen lay broken over a crushed shrub as if someone had jumped from the second floor. I took a series of pictures and walked cautiously through the flower bed, hoping to discover a clue.

"Can I help you?"

I froze and looked at a state police officer. "No. I was just looking around."

"Ms.?"

"Claudia Grant. I own Grant's Gowns next door. I was the one who found Mariah with the victim. You are?" I figured I would ask him a few questions, too.

"Trooper Anson." He scanned the area in the fading light. Seeming to take note of the screen, window, and state of the shrub. "Please step away from the bushes."

There was no mistaking his authority. I picked my way

from the house until I stood beside the trooper on the sidewalk. "For the record, I didn't see anything on the ground, and if you think I'd pick up a clue, you can ask Officer Jacobs; he'll vouch for my integrity."

His brow arched. "Good to know." With a sweeping gesture, he said, "Would you care to return inside?"

I held up my cell. "In just a minute, I need to let some people know we've been delayed. We're having leftovers at my place. I cooked dinner yesterday, and you know what that's like." I rambled on as if we weren't standing in front of evidence in a murder case.

"Fine. I'll wait for you." He took one step back.

"Oh. Okay." I tapped the speed dial button for Beth and gave him a tiny smile as if to say it wouldn't take long.

"Hey Beth, it's me."

"Claudia. I thought you were only going to be taking a quick trip to the inn. Is everything all right? I noticed a few police cars heading down Main Street. Any idea where they're going?"

"That's why I'm calling." I licked my lips and turned my back on the trooper. "There's been a murder at the inn. Gram and I walked in and discovered Mariah holding Andi McGinty's body. It seems she's been poisoned."

"No!"

"Yes," I whispered into the phone, "and I have pictures. Are you ready to start up the band again?" I glanced over my shoulder, hoping she'd get my meaning, mindful of Trooper Anson's intense focus on my every word.

"You're not alone?"

"No. Eddie and Rhonda are inside with two state troopers, and one officer is outside with me."

"Gotcha. You can't talk. What do you need from me?"

"I'm hoping Gram and I will leave in less than a half hour. Can you tell your dad there's been a change of plans and that dinner's at my place, but it's been delayed a bit? I'll call Mom and let her know, too."

"There's no need to call your mother. She and Dad just went to Polly's Pantry. I need cream for tomorrow. When they get back, I'll fill them in."

"Thanks. I'm not sure if Eddie will make it. I guess it depends on what he needs to do here. Right now, he's with the victim's brother."

"That stinks."

"For both men." I switched the phone to my other hand and spoke louder. "I'll see you at my place in a half hour."

"It's a plan."

I hung up. "Finished." His eyes followed me up the steps, and once the door closed behind me, with the trooper on the other side of the door, I exhaled.

Squaring my shoulders, I entered the lobby. Gram sat quietly with Mariah. I marveled at her patience.

She asked, "Were you able to reach Beth and your mom?"

"They're going to meet us at home in a half hour."

"Good."

"Where's Oliver?" There were numerous questions regarding where he had been for such a long time. Gram gave an almost imperceptible shake of her head, which silenced my questions.

"Claudia, I'm frightened. Should he be talking with the state troopers?" Mariah's eyes were brimming with tears as she wrapped her arms around her waist. "What if whatever was used to kill that poor girl is still in the inn? Anyone could ingest it and die."

I sank down beside her and took her cold, clammy hand in mine. Squeezing it, I said, "We can ask Eddie as soon as he's free. If there is any reason to be concerned, or if he feels you need to shut the inn down until the investigation is complete, he'll tell you."

"I wish Oliver was beside me."

Gram patted her arm. "He'll be finished very soon."

My head snapped up as the murmur of voices from the laundry room grew in intensity until I heard Shawn shout, "What do you mean we can't leave?"

Another exchange, and then he stormed past us and into the living room. "Guess what? We're stuck here until the investigation is closed. They think one of us killed my sister."

"What?" a female voice said.

I needed to know who said what.

I crept to the door, and Andi *whooshed* around me, hovering next to her brother. "Which one of you miscreants killed me?"

Eddie touched my arm, and I jumped back.

"What are you doing?" he asked.

Pressing a finger across my lips I whispered, "Trying to figure out who's outraged the most."

"Go home."

I shook my head. "Not until Oliver is finished with Trooper Stanton."

"How's Mariah holding up?" He kept an eye on the fam and friend group even if he was asking questions about Oliver and Mariah.

"Not good."

Over Eddie's radio, I heard Rhonda's voice. "Oliver Jones requests to speak with you. I'll escort him to the kitchen."

"Copy that." He said, "Go home, Gigi. And stay out of this case. Whoever killed Andi McGinty doesn't play nice. Poison is a nasty way to die."

I gave him a penetrating gaze, hoping to see what hovered behind those blue-gray eyes. There was something he wasn't saying. "Murder's always bad."

He gave me a brisk nod. "True. Now, go. I'll swing by your apartment as soon as I can."

"Please be gentle with Mariah. This has been a shock, and initially she had to handle it without her husband's support."

"I'll be kind." He nodded toward the door. "Please?"

"What is it you don't want me to see?"

He threw up his hands. "Everything. They're going to remove the body soon and trust me, you don't want to be here."

"Five minutes?" My gaze darted to Mariah. "She's vulnerable and she shouldn't see the body being taken out, either."

Pointing toward where she sat, I asked, "Do you have any idea how it happened? Mariah's worried it could happen to someone else if there's been cross-contamination."

"We found a water bottle that had rolled under the table. Trooper Ryan believes that's the method of delivery. Obviously, we can't be sure until tests are conducted. In addition, there'll be a team here combing every square inch of the inn tonight. If there's a source other than the water bottle, we'll find it."

"Do you think you'll find more than Andi's fingerprints on the bottle?"

"I'm sure." He said, "I need to get in the other room and ask some questions. You'll be on your way very soon, right?"

I had heard that tone of voice before and he was serious even if he sounded like a broken record. "Yes."

"Mariah!"

"Oliver," came out as a cry. She was halfway to the kitchen door with her arms wide.

Wrapping his arms around her, holding tight, he said, "I'm so sorry, sweetheart. I just told the officer I zipped down to Portland to pick up something. Forgive me that I wasn't here when everything happened?" He stepped back and took her face between his hands. "Are you okay now?"

She nodded, pressing her cheek to his. "Claudia and her grandmother found me shortly after I discovered Andi on the floor. They called the police and didn't leave me."

He broke eye contact with her. "Claudia, what can you tell me?"

Rhonda cleared her throat. "Mr. Jones. As an ongoing investigation, I must insist you direct all questions to the proper authorities. Claudia and her grandmother just happened on the scene and comforted your wife."

I remained silent, allowing Rhonda to create the illusion of her own importance. One of these days, I'd figure out what she had against me.

Today was not that day.

Rhonda said, "I need to ask you additional questions at the station."

Mariah's face paled and Oliver's Adam's apple bobbed in his throat. "As in the police station?"

She arched a brow. "Yes. Is that a problem?"

He wrapped his arm around Mariah's waist and held her close to his side. "I don't want to leave my wife."

"She's coming too, as will the rest of Ms. McGinty's friends and family. This will allow the crime scene experts to do their job while I do mine."

"And then what happens? Will we be able to return to the inn?"

"Yes, we believe we can clear the rooms for the other guests and, of course, your apartment; however, the laundry room and room four will be sealed and off-limits to everyone."

Oliver clutched Mariah's hand. "We understand."

"Rhonda, if you'd prefer, I can have my family stay with me for a few days."

"Thank you, Claudia. It's not necessary."

"Officer Perkins, my daughter and I have adjoining rooms. Would it be possible for me to stand in the door while you searched our rooms?

"Mrs. Grant, your rooms have been searched already, and you're free to return to them whenever you wish." She gave my grandmother a kind smile—something I hadn't associated with the newcomer to the Drakes Bay police force.

"Thank you, Officer. We'll be at Claudia's for dinner."

As I watched the exchange, I wondered what special magic my grandmother employed to make Rhonda nice. That was a skill I needed to cultivate.

"Mariah, if you and Oliver need anything, please call or drop by. I have plenty of leftovers, too, if you're hungry."

She grimaced. "I don't think I could eat a bite, but we appreciate the offer."

Oliver nodded his thanks.

"It's an open invite if you change your mind." All remaining words evaporated as I noticed Rhonda's frown. My stalling tactic wasn't working. As morbid as it sounded to my ears, I wanted to see if any of the friends would charge into the lobby and say something—anything—that could indicate who killed this poor girl. "We're leaving."

The newest ghost on the block drifted over. "You're leaving me? I'll have no one to talk to."

Gram said, "Let's go outside."

That was for Andi's benefit, not mine. Rhonda's eyes followed us as we left, and the ghost drifted along with us.

When the door closed, Gram waved to Andi. "Come as far as you can, and we'll talk."

"How will I know how far I can go?"

"It'll be like running into a brick wall." Gram's steps were quick over the stone walk to the parking area.

Andi floated along behind her until she stopped suddenly. "I'm stuck."

"Now we know your boundary—at least for now. If we don't solve your murder and you cross over, more than likely, you'll be stuck inside the inn until your death is resolved."

"I don't like how that sounds. I'm afraid of ghosts and things that go bump in the night. What if there are others, and they don't like me?" Her head dropped. "No one does."

"Andi, what do you mean by that?"

She looked over her shoulder at the inn. "I'm only with

them because my brother said if I wasn't welcome on the extended vacation, he wasn't coming, either."

"You're not all friends?"

She shook her head. "I wish. They barely tolerate me."

This just cracked the investigation wide open.

"I take that back. Clark has always been nice to me. He and Shawn were friends since grade school. He used to tease me back then. I'm a year younger. Was a year younger." Ghostly tears welled up in her eyes. "I'm never going to get old."

"Would you say that Clark was your friend?"

"At one time, but that was B.A."

"I don't understand."

"Sorry; it was an inside joke between me and Shawn. Before Ava. Once they started dating, Clark ignored me as much as possible, and when they got married, it became much worse. Ava hated me and the history I had with Clark. It wasn't like we dated for very long, just a couple of months —why can't we just be old friends?"

"Could an old rivalry be the reason you were poisoned?"

"If you want to point the finger at someone, Pixie would be the more logical choice. And if she's looking to eliminate competition for Clark's affections, then Ava will be the next to die. But if she wanted a relationship with Shawn— Not like he'd let that happen. He sees right through her." She held her shimmering hand to her face. "Ironic huh? He can see through her, but he can't see me."

8

There wasn't anything more to learn from Andi. Gram and I walked through the alley to my building.

"Jealousy is one of the main reasons for murder." I took Gram's arm as we ascended the stairs.

She said, "Motives are plentiful in this case: revenge for what a person could perceive as a past wrong, jealousy, as you said, financial gain, and maybe fear."

We reached the top step. The lights were on inside, and I paused. "I don't think money is the motivation; they all appear to be wealthy."

"Appearances are often what a person wants to project. It might not be reality." She pulled the door open. "Keep an open mind."

"How do you know so much about crime?" I followed her inside.

"You know I adore reading Agatha Christie over and over. That's where my love of mystery began." She gave me a side glance. "Have you ever read the book, *Amateur Sleuth Society*?"

"No, should I?"

"Yes, but the bigger point is that I belong to a group fashioned after that book, and we examine famous historical true-life cases to try and solve them. It's a good workout for the brain cells."

I shrugged off my coat and took Gram's, hanging them in the closet.

A twinkle appeared in her eye. "There are a great many details about your old grandmother that you don't know. This weekend might be eye-opening for you. Talking to ghosts and mystery is just the tip of the iceberg."

Mom rushed around the corner, her face drawn and pale. "You're home." She threw her arms around us. "Beth told me what happened, and I've been worried. So, Ethan used his key to let us in. I hope you don't mind."

"Of course not, Mom. I'm glad you're here and I'm sorry that you were concerned. We were perfectly safe. Whatever occurred was directed at the victim."

She hugged us even tighter. "I don't like it. Maybe you should move home?"

I wriggled from her arms and walked into the living room. "What happened had nothing to do with me. Besides, Drakes Bay is my home. I love it here and I have no plans on leaving."

Beth hurried over and hugged me tight. "That's good to hear but I'm sorry about Andi McGinty."

Perched on his usual window ledge, Herman waved to me. "I can't wait to hear the details."

Mom and Gram were on my heels, and Gram covered a giggle with a cough. "Would someone mind getting me a glass of water?"

Ethan said, "I'll get it for you, Erma."

"How about tea or perhaps coffee?" Mom asked.

I held up my hand like a school kid in class. "Wine for me."

Beth smiled. "I'll second that."

"Let's hit the wine cellar." I crossed to the door leading to the shop. "We'll be right back." I flicked the light on and hurried down the steps. At the bottom, I repeated the process, going into the basement. Once we entered the wine room, I closed the door. No one was going to overhear our conversation. The most important part I couldn't tell her was that the victim was now a ghost.

As soon as we were behind the closed door, Beth asked, "What happened?"

"Gram and I were going over to get her new skirt, as she wanted to freshen up a bit before dinner. When we walked inside, Mariah screamed for help. We found her on the laundry room floor, holding Andi McGinty in her arms."

"She feel for a pulse and then call for help?"

"No." I shrugged, "My guess? Shock."

She nodded. "I get that. I remember when we found Colton Prescott on the floor. Other than feeling for a pulse, we were both instantly numb to everything."

"In a bizarre twist, Gram's new skirt was draped around her neck like some kind of fashion statement. Eddie's sure it was poison, so I'm concluding there weren't any strangulation marks on her neck."

"Then why incorporate the skirt at all?"

"She might have had it in her hands? We know she left her friends to return to the inn to get her medicine." *Wait,* did her brother say that, too? Or was it just Andi's ghost who told me? It was going to get confusing obtaining information in the usual way as well as from a ghost.

"Then why didn't they come looking for her sooner? You were over there for at least a half hour, and if she was already dead when Mariah found her, that was a long time to just run over to get something. Drakes Bay isn't that big."

"A point I hadn't thought about." I pulled my phone from my pocket, tapped in the passcode, and handed it to her. "Gram got as many pictures as she could."

She scrolled through them. "Holy cannoli, her room is a disaster. Do you think she left it like that?"

"No, the window was open, and the screen was pushed out. I've got photos toward the end of the broken bushes. It was deliberate."

She handed me the phone. "We need to talk to the other five and see who left the group in town while Andi returned to the inn."

"That's what I was thinking. Oh, and her coat and handbag are missing."

"How do you know that?"

"She wasn't wearing a jacket. Based on the pictures of her room, they weren't there. So, what happened to them? And this morning, when I watched her go to her room after the juice incident, she stumbled at the top and grabbed the banister and then the wall to steady herself. Could it have been possible she was being slowly poisoned with the final dose pushing her to her death?"

"You said she was dealing with a migraine—that could make her unsteady."

"Headaches are also a symptom of poisoning."

"Did you mention any of this to Eddie?" Beth asked.

"Not yet. You know I like to organize my thoughts instead of spinning a theory. I'm sure he's already questioning the friends and her brother about where they were during the hour she wasn't with them and why it took them so long to come after her."

She said, "That will be a question at the start of the conversation, what time did she leave the group? Now, looking back, did she seem upset or anything to cause them to be concerned? Each person will be asked those questions so there will be five different observations."

"I wish we could be there when they question everyone, including Mariah and Oliver. There's one important clue I forgot to mention. One of the troopers found an open water bottle under the table. It's going to be tested for poison."

After randomly selecting a few bottles of wine, she said, "That's too obvious. It won't be the delivery method for the final dose. There must be something in her handbag, which is why it's missing. The killer is trying to find whatever was dosed."

Herman drifted in. "Don't let her take those bottles upstairs. They're not appropriate for leftovers. Take items from the rack marked E.D."

"Beth, would you mind if I selected a couple of different bottles?"

Her eyes widened momentarily before she smiled. "No problem. I just grabbed them. I have no idea what's good or not."

"They're all excellent," Herman groused.

I selected two distinct wines and a total of four bottles from the E. D. rack.

Taking a closer look, she asked, "What does the *E* and *D* stand for?"

"Tell Beth, these are everyday wines—more casual."

Now, that makes sense. Going off the cuff, I responded, "This rack is for casual drinking. My uncle collected wine for a variety of reasons—special dinners, casual meals, for sangria, and sipping."

"Did he leave a guide or something?" She looked at the next rack. "Does P stand for poultry?"

He said, "Yes."

"It does." I pushed the door open before she asked more questions Herman needed to answer. "Will you get the light?"

She snapped it off and went in front of me. "I wish we could set up the board."

My mom and your dad would get upset, but when they leave after dinner, we will."

She laughed. "Exactly."

"As long as Eddie doesn't show up and put a damper on things."

"Worse would be if Rhonda stopped by. As usual, she was charming at the scene. Someday, I'll figure out why she doesn't like me."

"We know why. She holds a grudge that Eddie won't date her, and let's face it, he's only got eyes for you."

"I. No. He," I stammered.

She laughed. "Based on that reaction, you're interested in him, too. I knew it from the first time he referred to you as Gigi."

"A nickname means nothing."

"Right. Or the looks you each sneak in the other's direction when neither of you are paying attention." She tapped the corner of her eye. "I don't miss those longing glances. In fact, Luke and I are wondering how long it will take for the two of you to agree to a real date. Not hanging out with us on a double."

We reached the top of the basement stairs, and I secured the door. I had to divert this conversation—and fast. "Where's Luke tonight? I was hoping he'd come over for leftovers."

"He's still at his family's cabin on Bryant Pond. Each year the Devlins gather for Thanksgiving and then, starting tomorrow, they'll winterize the cabin. It's late in the season but a tradition they love."

"Sounds nice. But chilly. The winds off the water are wicked, and what if it snows?"

"They plow their way in from the town road. It's quite an adventure." She had a wistful tone in her voice.

"Maybe next year you'll be spending the holiday on Bryant Pond, too."

With a shake of her head, she said, "Not likely. I need to have the shop open on Friday. Besides, I won't leave Dad alone on any holiday. I'm all he has besides Eddie."

"That's understandable. Before we go up, I want to show

you how much of your inventory I sold today." A few spotlights on the windows softly lit the shop. The table Beth had artfully arranged with knitwear, from sweaters to mittens and scarves, was empty.

Scanning the room, she asked, "Did you move the display?"

I grinned. "Nope, and the inventory I have left in the back is two cardigans and a few hats. Otherwise, you sold out!"

Her hand flew to her mouth. "Are you kidding me?"

"You're a hit!"

"*We're* a hit. Did you sell skirts and slacks with each sweater purchase?"

"Sure did. I don't know what you have in inventory or if any of your knitters has a stash, but I could use more product before opening tomorrow."

Hugging me tightly, she said, "I'll be over at eight. Dad can help, and if you need stuff brought out of storage, we can help with that, too."

"Slow down, partner. I want us to be strategic. We have a full month of shoppers to satisfy."

It was like she didn't hear me. "Tomorrow, I'll call my knitters and see what we can get in each color palette and size range. Were there any issues with sizing, such as was there any one size or style that sold quickly?"

"Cardigans sold fast—and the larger sizes. Smalls were slower to move, but they still sold. We need everything."

"Here's what I'll do." She scanned the room. "First thing tomorrow, I'll come over and we can discuss what might sell for the rest of the weekend, and plan what we need for the next four weeks. The last thing we want is excess inventory after the holidays when we're starting on the spring collection, but we need more now. Toward the end of December, we'll stock a few pieces that would transition to warmer months or that folks can take on vacation. What do you think?"

"That'll work, but I need to whip up some slacks and skirts, so we'll need to coordinate that transition line."

"Agreed." She held up her hand and slapped me a high five. "I have to admit, hoping this would take off isn't the same as seeing it happen." A breath escaped her lips. "What if today was a fluke?"

I laughed. "If you could have heard the comments from the shoppers, that thought wouldn't have crossed your mind. Since we're both closing at three on Sunday, would you like to design a few pieces and work through dinner? I'll print flyers advertising our new spring clothes and put them in bags with each purchase."

Her smile widened. "That's a fantastic idea. Save a stack for me."

"It's settled. We'll meet here at eight tomorrow, and Sunday… Wait. We can't have a working supper. Mom's cooking dinner for everyone at your dad's place."

"We'll ask Dad to have dinner at seven, and we can still work for an hour, go to the park for the tree lighting, come back here for an hour and then dinner."

"Do you think he'll mind? I can ask Mom and Gram too."

"Dad'll support us, so absolutely not. And the upside is that your family will have fun while we work. Hopefully they're okay with a slight time change."

"Beth, I'm thrilled you brought this idea up a few months ago. Getting inventory on the shelves and organized has been a whirlwind, but it's not just good for our businesses. As you said, it's good for ladies in town who love to knit as it's giving them income as well."

"Don't go getting all serious on me, Grant. This is better than hoping to sell a few items at a craft fair which is what they've done in the past."

Her focus strayed to the front window. "Don't look now, but isn't that the people from the inn standing at the entrance to the park?"

I felt a cool breeze on my face. My overly protective ghost was beside me. "Don't go out there."

Tempers must be hot. As Shawn spoke, his arms flailed through the air. There was little traffic on the street; maybe his voice would carry. I crept to the window, leaned into the display to ease it open. Beth mirrored my action with the other casement window.

Shawn's voice drifted to us. "What do you mean Andi never fit in? Are you happy she's dead?" He took a menacing step toward Pixie. "You're a cold, heartless..."

Ava grabbed his arm and glared at Pixie. "This is getting us nowhere. Grief is running rampant, and people are saying things they don't mean."

He shook off her hand. "All I'm asking is where were Hugo and Pixie after Andi went back to the inn? We must walk into that police station and be brutally honest with every detail. And I won't hold back and tell them that the two of you," he jabbed a finger into Hugo's chest and leered at Pixie, "were missing for at least thirty minutes."

Pixie glared at Ava. "Don't forget before that Ava had wandered off, saying she wanted to visit the dress shop."

A car drove by, muffling Ava's response, but I noticed she stamped her foot. Then, she grabbed her husband's hand and shouted, "Clark will vouch for me."

He withdrew his hand and shoved it into his jacket pocket. I glanced at Beth and nodded. Would he give his wife an alibi?

Herman said, "Body language is critical in this instance. All but the man in the tan coat, who's devastated, are on the defensive. Is that the victim's brother?"

"Shawn's not the killer. Look at his posture; slumped shoulders rounded in as if protecting himself, like he couldn't keep his sister safe. Right now, it could be any of the remaining four who killed Andi."

9

———

 eth and I waited until the group disappeared into the park. I closed the window, and she did the same. I said, "They must be cutting through the park on their way to the police station."

"I'm surprised Rhonda didn't give them a ride."

I couldn't help but smile. "I'm sure she wanted to, but they obviously wanted time alone before walking in. Do you think Shawn hoped one would confess to the deed before they got to the police station?"

"Wishful thinking," Herman said before he zipped from the room.

"That put a damper on my fun. The reality that a young woman lost her life today is sobering, and to think one of the so-called friends had something to do with it makes it even worse."

She gave me a thoughtful look. "Do you have a guess as to the motive?"

Sitting on the display's edge, I contemplated the day's events. "Jealousy or revenge is my bet. They all appear to be wealthy, so money wouldn't be a motive. However, it was pointed out to me that appearances could be deceiving." I withdrew my phone and scanned the pictures of Andi's room, pausing to enlarge the image of her makeup bag. "These cosmetics are expensive." I turned the phone around so Beth could look.

"If I know my yarns, that baby blue sweater in a heap is cashmere. It's too bad I can't see the label; I could give you a better idea of the grade."

"It would be more helpful if we could look into the suspects' backgrounds. Are they who they say?" Standing up, I pulled Beth to her feet. "When we set up the murder board, we're going to conduct an internet search on each person, including Shawn and Andi. That should give us some insight into the motive of at least one of them."

She rubbed her hands together. "Sofa sleuths are back in action."

I laughed. "I might clue my grandmother in on what we're up to. Apparently, she's part of a group that loves reviewing real mysteries, but at least what they work on are old and very cold cases. So, they're less likely to encounter a living culprit."

"Go, Erma."

Toss in the tidbit of talking to ghosts and my grandmother could be an asset for anyone trying to solve a crime. However, I was keeping her away from this one. Far away.

I leaned back in my chair and rubbed my protruding tummy. "How is it possible I just ate two slices of pie in addition to a full plate of leftovers?"

Gram gave me an indulgent smile. "Thanksgiving comes once a year, my dear girl, and you made a delicious dinner. I can start the stock tonight and whip up a pot of soup for our lunch tomorrow if you'd like."

"You don't have to work. I'll do it."

Gram's eyes widened.

Oh, I knew that look and she wasn't happy that I turned down her offer. "But if you want, my kitchen is yours."

Beth grinned. "You had me at soup—that's if there's enough."

Mom laughed. "Erma will make enough soup to feed us all for several meals."

A sharp knock on the door drew my attention. "Eddie said he was stopping over." I pushed the chair back and stood.

He waved at me through the glass door, dressed in jeans and a heavy winter jacket.

"Hey, you. Come in. Are you hungry?"

"I could eat if you still have leftovers." He leaned in like he was going to kiss my cheek but pulled back and averted his eyes.

"How were things at the station?"

Handing me his jacket, he toed off his Blundstone boots. "Chaos. The brother mentioned a few important clues."

"That Pixie and Hugo disappeared for over thirty minutes, and Ava doesn't have an alibi around the same time since Clark won't say he was with her?"

His gaze leveled on me. "If I didn't know better, I'd say you bugged the station."

"That would be a bad idea, Eddie." I gave him a tentative smile. "I'm sure there's a law against it."

"Get that gleam out of your eye. I'm sorry I mentioned it —and for the record, there *is* a law. How do you know the details of our conversations?"

"The five of them were across the street at the park entrance. Beth and I were in the shop reviewing inventory. I had a great day and sold out of most of the knitwear. We were talking about our plan for the morning when we noticed them."

"Please tell me you didn't go out and ask questions."

"Of course not. That's a sure way to get them to clam up.

Instead, Beth and I opened the casement windows and listened. Sound travels in the cold and there was little traffic, except one car drove by when Ava was proclaiming her innocence."

"Do you think they saw you?"

I shook my head. "Doubtful. I didn't have many lights on, and they weren't looking around; just arguing—and Shawn was so upset. He's devastated by what happened. Oh, and Pixie made the comment that Andi never fit into the group. That's when Shawn blasted her, asking if his sister deserved to die."

He cocked a brow. "That is interesting. I wonder why she didn't fit in."

It was on the tip of my tongue to tell him that Clark and Shawn had been friends for years, but there was no way I could know that information. "Have you checked into their backgrounds? Did they go to school together? Perhaps college?"

"Clark, Shawn, and Andi grew up together. I'm not sure when or where they met the others."

"Interesting."

He placed a hand on my shoulder. "You need to forget about this case and stay focused on your dress shop. Between the MSP, Rhonda, and me, we'll close the case."

"What about Mariah and Oliver? They're crushed."

"They're not suspects. She had the unfortunate luck of finding Andi, and there are trauma specialists she can speak with. Oliver was steady as a rock."

"Where was he? Portland?"

"He's been cleared. We've verified he was buying a present for Mariah; there's even footage of him at the store. He'd like to keep that a secret if possible, and as far as we're concerned, there's no issue with protecting his privacy."

My mind raced. "What about the white powder behind the counter that one trooper investigated."

"Powdered sugar. Satisfied?" He bobbed his head toward the apartment's interior and a twinkle sparkled in his eyes. "If you're done grilling me, can we go in? I'm sure everyone is wondering what we're doing out here."

I stepped back and swallowed hard at the tiny flirtatious comment. Or was it? "Sure."

"Hello, all. Sorry I'm late." Eddie pulled out a chair across from where I had been sitting. "Busy day."

Mom said, "Eddie, if you fix a plate, I'll heat it in the microwave for you."

He gave her a warm smile. "Thanks, Dana. You don't need to wait on me. I can do that."

"Mom, I'll heat it up for him." I poured him a glass of wine without asking if he'd like one. I said, "Are you off duty for the rest of the night?"

"Yes, ma'am. Pour away."

With bowls of food surrounding the table, he filled a plate and stood. "Gigi, I've got this. You can relax."

Mom's head spun from Eddie making himself at home in the kitchen to me. With a tip of her head, she asked a hundred questions—none of which I intended to answer.

My grandmother said, "Dana, leave the girl alone."

"Thanks, Gram."

She gave me a conspiratorial wink. "I do like him," she whispered.

The microwave beeped. Eddie returned with his plate. "I hate to eat in front of everyone, but I'm starved." Once he sat, he looked around. "Tell me, how was business today?"

Beth said, "Brisk. I had shoppers looking to get yarn for projects and sold ten beginner kits, but the biggest news: Claudia and my new partnership seems to be a hit. At least for one day."

"I heard. Gigi said you sold out in her shop." He gave me a sidelong glance and smiled. "The two of you are going to take over the fashion world."

Heat flushed my cheeks. "Just a tiny corner of Maine."

Gram tapped the top of the table. "I'm confident you'll expand beyond this part of the state. You'll get online orders once I start wearing my outfit at home. Are you prepared for that venture?" Her smile faded. "No offense, my darling girl, but I'll need to purchase a new skirt. There's no way I could wear the one that was draped around that unfortunate young woman."

"Gram, you can select anything you want from the store as my Christmas gift."

"Claudia, you can't give away profits. I insist on paying. Dana bought the first skirt." She gave my mother a stern look. "You did pay for the items?"

"Of course. Claudia did give me a slight discount." She shifted in her chair. "I can design a website if you'd like."

"Mom, that would be helpful. I have a home page but nothing else. Do you know how we can set up orders since inventory changes often?"

Ethan remained silent during the conversation until the inventory word came up. "I've been thinking Knit or Purl should have a website. Dana, if you are open to doing another, could I hire you to design one for Beth's business?"

She kicked me under the table and tipped her head between her dad and my mom.

"I'd be happy to discuss it with you. Maybe tomorrow we could talk about it when we go to the Italian market?"

He smiled. "We can do the market on Sunday if you're interested in drinks after the shop closes? If you're up for an adventure, we could drive up to Robins Pointe and go to the Magical Moonshine Pub. It has craft beers and great food."

"Well, I'd love to." She looked at the rest of us. "Would you care to join us?"

I shook my head. "I'll be exhausted after another hectic day in the store."

Beth said, "Me too."

Gram laughed, "You don't need four extra wheels on your date. Go and have fun."

Mom stuttered. "It's. Not…"

Ethan said, "I'd like to consider it our first date. Sorry everyone, for asking Dana out in front of you, but when inspiration strikes…" He gave Eddie a pointed look.

"Have fun. Dana, their Shandygaff with pale ale and ginger beer is excellent."

"In that case, Ethan, I accept." Color pinked her cheeks, and it had been a long time since she looked like a younger version of herself. Why she hadn't dated after my dad died was another mystery, but one I didn't want to talk about if she didn't want to bring it up.

Gram yawned. "It's been an eventful day. Would anyone care to walk me back to the inn?" She bobbed her head at my mom. "Dana?"

"I'll walk with you, Erma." She stacked the empty plates.

"Mom, I'll clean up." I winked at Ethan. "Would you mind accompanying the ladies, Ethan?"

"It would be my pleasure. Perhaps we could have a nightcap in the bar—or a cup of tea?"

Before Mom or Grandma could voice a concern, Eddie said, "The inn is safe. We found no evidence of any poison on the premises. In fact, Mariah uses baking soda and vinegar or non-toxic cleaners throughout the inn, and the gardens are also organically maintained."

Mom smiled at Ethan. "A drink in the bar sounds lovely. Erma, you're welcome to join us."

"We'll see." Gram stood and leaned over the table to kiss my cheek and whispered, "Have fun dissecting the clues, and I'll try to speak with Andi. I'll text if I learn anything from her."

That little minx wasn't tired, but she wanted to dive into the case, too. "Goodnight, Gram. Text me later."

"Don't worry about starting the stock for soup. I'll zip

over in the morning and do it. Just put everything on the deck overnight, but make sure the lids are secure. We don't need our four-legged friends helping themselves."

Eddie took another roll and buttered it. "Actually, there was a report of a bear a couple nights ago, so you don't want to leave any food on the deck overnight."

With a nervous laugh, I glanced at Ethan and Beth. "Can they climb stairs?"

She asked, "Does Yogi love picnic baskets?"

I gulped. "Okay, then. Gram, when you come over tomorrow, meet me in the store, and you can go in through the inside steps."

"Claudia, I doubt the bear will be waiting for me." She patted my cheek. "But I'll come to the shop. While I'm there, I can pick out a new skirt. Goodnight, darling."

Quickly, everyone put on their coats, and after a flurry of hugs, the trio left.

I strolled into the dining area. Beth had cleared the table, and Eddie was wolfing down a slice of pumpkin pie.

"I appreciate you feeding me tonight. It was a tough day."

"It was my pleasure, Eddie."

Beth had pulled what we called our "murder board" out of the hall closet and set up in front of the television. Herman had been scarce all evening, but now he reclined on the back of the sofa. I hadn't been able to tell him about Andi's ghost.

Eddie cleared his throat. "Does this mean you and Beth are going to talk about the murder of Andi McGinty?"

"So it would seem." I picked up my wine glass and said, "Care to join us?"

"Gigi, you know I can't comment on an ongoing investigation."

"She didn't ask you to, cuz. Do you want to stay and see what she might have observed that could help your case?"

Leave it to Beth to cut to the heart of the matter. "Grab another slice of pie and come sit."

He didn't hesitate this time. Cutting a generous slice of apple and a sliver of mince, he picked up a coffee mug and sat next to Beth.

In the center, I drew a circle and wrote "Andi McGinty." Then I drew five arrows coming from the circle and added "Shawn," "Pixie," "Hugo," "Ava," and "Clark." Underneath that, I wrote "POISON," and in the bottom right of the board, I added "Mariah" and "Oliver."

I stated, "Time of death was roughly three o'clock." I looked at Eddie who didn't say anything. I continued, "Andi. Early in the day stumbled up the stairs and grabbed the wall for stability. Migraine."

It was stilted, but this was just a clue board, not a written assignment. "After she and the group leave the inn, she returns for more medicine(?). If you are dealing with a migraine, wouldn't you either skip the sightseeing or take it with you?"

Beth said, "What if she felt better and figured she'd knocked it down but it boomeranged?"

"Good point." I wrote boomerang on the board under Andi's name. "Or was the dose she took earlier laced with poison and it made her symptoms worse. When she returned to the inn, she ingested the final dose which ended her life."

Eddie set his plate aside. "Then how and why did the skirt get draped around her neck?"

10

I flopped on the sofa next to Eddie and groaned. "What was the method of ingestion? Once that's known, it will be easier to determine who slipped it to Andi." It was a rhetorical question since he wouldn't know until the autopsy results were ready—and even then, he wouldn't tell me, but my frustration mounted. I wished Andi could remember what happened right before she collapsed.

Beth asked, "Do you think Andi knew something was terribly wrong?"

Picking up my wine glass, I sipped. "If she was a person who lived with headaches and the occasional feeling of malaise, she might have thought it was just another poor health day and dismissed the symptoms. I could ask Shawn her general state of health."

Eddie shook his head. "No, you won't. Leave the questions to the police."

"We know that people tend to talk more freely to someone who isn't a cop. What harm would it cause?"

"Plenty. You really want to push Rhonda's buttons? She'd love to arrest you for interfering."

"Have you told her that we're friends?"

His brow wrinkled. "Why would I? It's not relevant to my job."

"Maybe she'd lighten up. It's obvious she wants to date you. If she knew where our relationship stood, maybe she'd stop seeing me as a threat to her personal happiness."

Beth's eyes widened.

His lips thinned. "I'm not interested in dating her."

"Have you told her straight out that you won't date a co-worker?" Beth asked.

"When she started working at the station, I mentioned dating co-workers wasn't a good idea." He shifted on the sofa. "Did I need to be direct and say I wasn't interested? That would be rude."

"Until you do, she'll have hope that she can win you over. Remember, you don't have to be unkind, just direct."

Frowning, he looked at Beth and then his gaze lingered on me. "This will be an uncomfortable conversation."

Lola strutted across the floor and jumped into my lap. She had a trail of cobwebs running down her back. "Where have you been, little girl?"

Meow. Purrrr.

Herman put his face in hers. "I think she's found access to the attic."

"Eddie, I almost forgot. We were going to go into the attic tonight, but do you think we could do it early tomorrow?"

"Right, for the decorations. I'm not working the weekend, so I can swing by and help. Just name the time."

"Even with the investigation?"

Lola rolled onto her back, belly up, for me to rub her paws.

"I'll be poking around a bit but off the official clock." I tapped my chin thinking of spare time I didn't have. "You know, let's do it right now. The three of us can make quick work of it."

Beth jumped up. "I love creepy spaces."

Laughing, I placed Lola on the sofa. "You stay put."

Herman said, "I'll make sure she does."

"Too bad Herman wasn't here to tell me which boxes were for the shop and which were for the apartment."

"I know what you're doing, Claudia—and everything is clearly labeled. It'll be nice to see the space decorated; last year, the place was depressing." The melancholy tone in my sweet ghost's voice constricted my heart.

"I'm sure you can mix and match to your hearts content." Eddie pulled down the ladder in the front hall, and the trap door opened. "Claudia, grab that large flashlight at the top of the stairs. It'll be helpful if the overhead lights aren't bright enough."

Herman lingered near the downstairs door, and I whispered, "Anything I should know about the attic?"

"It has a great view of the inn. You might find it useful."

With a nod, I said, "We need to talk later. The victim became a ghost." I pulled the flashlight from the holder on the wall.

"That's very interesting."

Beth called, "Claudia, are you coming?"

He waved me toward the hall. "Go."

I rounded the corner with a smile. "Sorry, it was stuck." I handed the light to Eddie. "Are you going first?"

"Yes. The last time I helped Herman, the light chain was pretty short. I should replace it at some point in case you have to go up there by yourself." He scrambled up the ladder, and light filled the space.

I went next, with Beth following me. The space was huge. The ceiling was at least twelve feet, and the shelves lining the walls were clearly marked, much like the wine cellar. "Herman was very organized; finding what we need won't take long."

Eddie went to the red totes and placed several on the floor while Beth opened them. Glancing over my shoulder, I remembered Herman's comment about the view of the inn and the possible water leak. I wandered to the bank of windows facing the bay, which showcased the inn and Twice Loved. Light glowed in the second-floor windows. One room had its window cracked open. That must be Andi's. I looked at the screen still in the bushes. The rooms on either side were dark.

"Eddie, was everyone released from the police station?"

"Yes." He crossed the wide plank floor and stopped next to me. "You might have a leak. See? The wood on the wall is darker under the window. Give Beau a call and have him check it out."

"I will, thanks."

He gazed out the window. "Why did you ask about the others?"

"Just curious why they didn't go back to the inn."

"What makes you say they didn't?"

I pointed to the building. "The rooms on either side of Andi's are dark. If I had just been questioned, the only place I'd want to be is in my room, away from everyone. Especially Shawn. He must realize one of his so-called friends killed his sister."

Beth sat back on her heels, pausing as she sorted the decorations on the opposite side of the room, "Or he did."

"You saw him, Beth, on the street. You can't fake that depth of grief."

"He's grieving, but he could be responsible, although it's unlikely." Eddie said, "What's going on here?"

I turned. "What's that pinprick of light?" It slid from the floor up in a vertical pattern. "Someone's in Andi's room!"

He withdrew his phone. After a moment, which seemed like a day he said, "Rhonda. I'm in Claudia Grant's attic and noticed someone is in Andi McGinty's room."

He paused. "A small flashlight or maybe a cell phone. We

need backup there pronto. I'm not armed so I don't want to go in alone."

Another pause while he bobbed his head. "Right. I'll meet you outside."

He slid his phone into his pocket. "I gotta go. Stay here."

"We will." He dashed to the ladder and disappeared. The deck door slammed shut, as I remained focused on the inn and room four.

Beth gave me a playful shoulder bump. "Why do we have to go over there when we have a great view of what's happening right here? And nobody can tell us to stop looking out your window."

"Exactly. We might not be able to hear what's happening, but if someone should try to slip out a door or window, we'll see who it is."

The light continued to bounce around the room. "Whoever's in there is searching for something." I hoped Andi was close by to share the details with me.

This led me to my grandmother. Why hadn't she texted that she had talked with the new ghost? I couldn't call and ask her.

"Look. Eddie's skulking around the building." He stopped and looked up at the ajar window in what was Andi's room.

"Should we text him to say the person's still there?" I pressed my hand on the glass, scanning the area to make sure no one was sneaking up on him.

Beth shook her head. "If his phone's not silent, it could alert the intruder."

"Good point." My heart rate quickened as I saw a strobe of blue lights against the back of the building. "At least there isn't a siren."

Lights came on in the rooms flanking room four.

She asked, "Do you know who's staying there?"

"Other than Shawn, who's next door on one side or the other, I'm not sure. But Mariah can tell us in the morning."

"There's so much we don't know about this case besides whodunit. Motive and opportunity are at the top of the list, of course, but which one of the five had the most access to Andi, and how long would they have had to have been poisoning her before she succumbed?"

I looked at Beth. "Shawn would be the most likely if they hadn't all been together for the last week vacationing. Our murderer could have been slipping her the poison in small amounts to see how weak she'd become."

"And then, whammy!"

Tapping my chin, I considered the issue of the coat and shoulder bag. "Beth, if you were intent on killing someone and you snuck back to the inn either just before or right after the victim, why would you take their personal items and not leave them on the bench where they were?"

She cocked her head. "Why do you think they were there?"

Dang it. "It's where I'd drop them if I was running in to get something quick. Remember, she wasn't wearing a coat when Mariah found her. So, she'd have dropped it and most likely her bag too." *Did that sound plausible?*

"Good point. If we're going on the assumption Andi dropped her things near the entrance, are you sure they weren't in her room? She might have gone there first or the killer might have taken them upstairs. It would be less suspicious."

I pointed out the window. "Hold on. Who's that?"

"Where?" Beth leaned closer to the window. "I don't see anyone."

"A person is lying on the ground next to the bent screen."

"That's just the way the bushes are shadowing the ground."

Eddie glanced up at us before vanishing around the side of the house. Time crawled. The lights in room four flicked on. Shadows danced momentarily and then a body dove to the floor. Was that Eddie?

"What just happened?" she asked.

"My guess? Eddie and Rhonda entered the room. There was a tussle, and the perp is now under arrest." I wiped my sweaty palms on my slacks and stared at the person near the shrubs. If Beth couldn't see them, they must be a ghost.

She said, "Want to go to the deck to see who they're carting away in the cruiser?"

"Let's hurry. We can get the decorations later." I raced to the ladder and waited for Beth to climb down before pulling the overhead light chain and then following her. After folding the ladder, she handed me a jacket, and we walked out to the deck. From this vantage point, we had a clear line of sight to the inn's back door. Five minutes later, Rhonda came out, her hand clutching Hugo's bicep as she steered him into the backseat. She glanced at us after she closed the door and shook her head. There was little she could do since I was on my property.

"Hugo? I wasn't expecting him to search Andi's room." I leaned on the railing. "Feel like taking an evening stroll?" I gave her a side glance. "I haven't heard from Gram, and who knows? Maybe she's with Ethan and Mom enjoying a nightcap."

"Which means you think they could have witnessed what went on?"

"Maybe. What do you say?"

"Grab your keys and lock up." She grinned. "The sofa sleuths are changing location."

Once inside, I raced to the living room. "Herman, they've just arrested Hugo. Beth and I are going over to the inn. With some luck, I can bump into Andi." I snatched my keys from the counter. "Oh, do you know if there's another ghost living at the inn?"

Herman threw up his translucent arms. "How would I

know? Until recently, I didn't think I could go beyond these walls; now, I know the deck is an option. Even if I can't feel the warmth of the sun or smell the salty breeze, I remember how it was to enjoy life in this space."

I dropped my chin. "I'm being thoughtless, Herman. I'm sorry. Can you forgive me?" Even though I wanted to rush out the door, I waited patiently, giving my ghost time to consider my apology.

He rested his weightless hand on my arm. "Claudia, sometimes I forget that communicating with ghosts is new for you, too. While Erma is here, you should ask her some questions to understand how you can engage more."

As with so many moments during the last ten months, I wanted to hug Herman, but it wasn't possible. He'd slip through my arms and never feel my comforting warmth. "I'll do that but she mentioned she's never talked to a ghost until you. Will you be all right while I'm gone?"

"Of course. I was alone for months before you arrived. Maybe I can dream up a few designs for you. Once this unpleasantness of murder has concluded, I can describe my ideas, and you can put them into your little computer."

"Thanks, Uncle Herman. We shouldn't be gone long." I crossed the room and turned in the archway. "I know you might be ready to move to the afterlife, but I'm glad you're here."

He nodded, his smile sad. "Me too, Claudia. But do you know what you can do for the young ghost? Without someone to talk to every day, she'll be lonely. Solving this case so that she can move on will be best for her."

*B*eth and I raced down the steps. "What took you so long? I was about to go inside and make sure you hadn't been diverted by lemon pie."

"You do know my weakness, but I was remembering Andi

McGinty's sunny smile and I got sidetracked thinking how her life was ruthlessly cut short. She deserves justice, and I want us to help her get it so she can rest easy."

At the bottom step, Beth put her hand out to stop me. "She'll get justice. Eddie, Rhonda, and the Maine State Police will do their part."

"And we'll do our share of the heavy lifting. We're good at sourcing information, proving we have sharp minds for seeing through criminals' lies. Eddie can too, but our edge is we don't have to play by the rules of the job. We can ask questions, hang around, and appear to belong. Cops stand out and people get nervous around them. Until we find something that points to the killer, whether it's Hugo or one of the others, I want to be in the fray."

Where our passion for sorting through information came from was curious. "Beth, I'm glad we think alike. Now, go on inside, I want to take a quick peek under that window one more time before we start chatting up whoever's around since I was interrupted earlier by Trooper Anson."

She chewed the corner of her lip. "Are you sure it's safe? You were sure you saw someone loitering."

"I'll be fine." We split off and I went in search of a ghost. I just hoped it would be friendly.

11

———

*a*s I approached the side of the inn, where I was sure another ghost was lurking, goosebumps raced up my spine. I glanced over my shoulder.

"Boo!"

I screamed and jumped back, clutching the center of my chest, heart pounding. Floating in front of me was the translucent form of an older gentleman in a dark wool, tailored jacket, a high wing-collared shirt, a vest of a lighter shade than the jacket and pants, and a simply tied blue cotton cravat. "Who are you?"

He drifted back. "You can see me?"

"It's why I asked the question." I stepped forward. "Who are you?" I hated repeating myself, but in this instance, it was warranted.

"Mr. Thomas Pennington, owner and innkeeper of the Whistlers Inn." He took in my dark slacks and red puffer jacket. "And you are the young woman who lives next door?"

I narrowed my eyes. "How did you know that?"

"I often walk the grounds of my beloved inn and noticed you moved in some time ago." He drifted closer. "How is it you see me? No one has ever acknowledged my presence, at least not in a very long time."

"Are there a lot of ghosts in Drakes Bay?"

"Young lady, my haunting ground is my home. But since you're here and can talk to me, is there a possibility you can rid my establishment of that new ghost? I think she calls herself Andi, which is an inappropriate name for a lady. She's not welcome to stay here for eternity."

Andi was a topic I wanted to discuss, but we would get back to her in a few minutes. "Why are you here? Do you have unfinished business?"

"I'm here to watch over my establishment. No one can run it as well as I. Unfortunately, I took sick, and my wife was unable to nurse me back to health. I rallied at the end, and I was able to get dressed. It would be most undignified if I had to spend eternity in my nightshirt."

"You don't want to cross over to be with your loved ones?"

He crossed his arms and tapped his foot in mid-air. "Who would look after my inn?"

The indignation in his voice was surprising yet somehow expected. Herman had the same sense of ownership over the dress shop. "Well, if you change your mind, I might be able to help you with unfinished business so you could join your wife in the afterlife."

He bowed his head in a courtly manner. "Thank you, but no. I'm happy with the way things are. My distant relatives, Oliver and Mariah, are doing a fine job." With a glance at the open window, his face soured. "Except for that woman. She must go. Getting herself killed in my inn. What will that do to business?"

"That's why I'm here. My friend Beth and I want to help the police solve the crime." Crossing my fingers behind my back, I said, "Once Andi knows who killed her and why, she'll be happy to leave."

He narrowed his eyes and gave a thoughtful nod. "Then I will help you."

"Did you see who poisoned her?"

"No. I did not." He held up his hand as I opened my mouth. "But her friends have been arguing about how they didn't like the unfortunate girl but wished this hadn't happened to her poor brother. To not feel sorrow for the deceased is wrong."

"Mr. Pennington, what happened to her coat and bag?"

"Miss Grant, I can't be in every corner of the inn at the same time; however, I do know where the coat and her reticule have been secured.

"Her reticule? Oh, her purse. Right. And please, call me Claudia."

"Miss Grant, we don't know each other well enough for me to call you by your given name. It's not proper."

I smothered a laugh as I covered my mouth. "You're a ghost, and you've been dead for at least one hundred years. Times have changed, and it's perfectly acceptable for you to call me Claudia. May I call you Thomas?"

"You may." He zipped around the corner, leaving me speechless. He wasn't as nice as Uncle Herman's ghost—or even Andi's, for that matter.

Since I needed to get inside and still hadn't looked around, my intuition nagged at me even though I had been searching for the ghost and found him. There must be more going on out here—especially under the bush since that's where I discovered Thomas's ghost. I kneeled on the cold hard ground and turned on my flashlight app, lifting the shrubs as I crept along the perimeter of the bush.

A flash of metal glinted from the beam of light and a scrap of tan fabric almost obscured it. My fingers grazed the fabric when I heard a voice say, "Don't move."

My shoulders slumped toward the mulch. Rhonda? I

thought she took Hugo to the police station. I tipped my head to the side and stared into a bright blinding light.

"Claudia, open your eyes." Beth rubbed my hand in hers. My head throbbed so I kept them shut.

"I've called for the ambulance." Eddie's voice was soothing. "What was she doing out here by herself?" He laid something over me, and it smelled like his cologne.

"Eddie? What's happened?"

A crush of familiar voices began demanding answers simultaneously—a sharp whistle cut through the din.

"I don't know what's happened other than Claudia was hit on the head, and Beth found her unconscious. The ambulance will arrive shortly and transport her to the hospital."

Eddie had to look under the shrubs. I groaned. "Evidence. Buckle. Tan."

Beth squeezed my hand. "You found something?"

"Yes."

The blare of the siren cut through the darkness. I winced as the sound sliced through my brain. "Make it stop."

Beth said, "Dana, come over here."

She pulled away, and I felt Mom take my hand. "Claudia, honey, Ethan will drive me and Erma to the hospital."

"No need. Stay here. Beth will bring me home."

"Nonsense. I'm not sitting around this inn while you're in an emergency room."

I forced myself to open my eyes. Mom's eyes brimmed with tears. "It's just a bump. Nothing to worry about." Lifting my free hand, I pressed on the area where it hurt. A thick, sticky substance coated my fingertips. "Am I bleeding?"

She nodded. "Not to worry. We'll get you cleaned up."

"Excuse me, ma'am. If you'd step back. We need to assess the patient."

At least they didn't call me a victim. "Eddie, look under the bushes. Andi's coat and bag are there. I saw them."

Another EMT knelt beside me. "Can you tell me your name and what happened to you?"

"Claudia Grant. Someone hit me. I don't know who had the light, it blinded me."

"What day is it, the date, and who's president?"

I rattled off the information. It reminded me of when Fiona had been clobbered over the head. They thought I had a concussion. I tried to push myself to a sitting position. "I'm fine, just a couple of Band-aids and I'll be good."

"The doctor will be the judge. We'll get you on the gurney and have you checked out."

"I have things to do for tomorrow. Beth, tell them."

"Gigi, get checked out, a couple of stitches, and if the doc says it's okay, you can come home tonight, and I'll work in the shop for you tomorrow."

A frown crept over my lips. "You're going to work in a dress shop? Not likely."

He laughed, and after I was secured to the rolling cot, he leaned over and for my ears alone said, "I'll look for Andi's things. Get checked out and I'll see you soon."

I gazed into his clouded blue-gray eyes. "We're going to talk."

"I'll either come to the hospital or meet you at home."

My heart melted a little when he said home. "See you soon?"

He flashed a goofy little smile. "See you sooner."

My lips quirked. "That sounds nicer," and I closed my eyes.

True to his word, Ethan brought Mom and Gram to the hospital and then drove them back to my place while Beth volunteered to chauffeur me. I knew it was so we could talk about what happened between the time she went inside and when she found me.

"That's quite a lump on your head." Beth glanced at me. "Why were you out there so long?"

My fingertips grazed the thick bandage. "I'm positive I found Andi's missing coat and bag. And I only got three stitches and a mild concussion for my trouble."

"While the doctor was examining you, Eddie talked to Dad and me. Something had been dragged from under the shrubs. All that was left behind was a button. At this point, there's no way to confirm if it was attached to Andi's coat. He's got nothing to compare it to."

"Shawn might recognize it."

"Eddie's already asked him and the others. No one can say one way or the other."

I stared out the window. Andi's ghost would know. "Did Eddie take a picture of the button?"

With a laugh, she said, "You never give up, do you."

"Whoever was outside watching me took them. Were you in the bar?"

"Yes, with our family. The only person who joined us was Shawn. He sat by the fire nursing a drink."

I watched the road through the windshield. "He's off the suspect list for now."

"Maybe for attacking you, but not my list for killing Andi. I did a quick search on the internet while at the ER, and they're from a well-to-do family. With Andi gone, he will inherit everything when his parents pass away. Motive."

"Did you look up the others?" I carefully shifted in the passenger seat to face Beth.

"I sure did. Clark also comes from a wealthy family, but Ava married into it. As for Pixie and Hugo, I thought they were cousins, but they're not related at all. If you lie about that, what else are you lying about?"

"Are you sure?"

"Very. I dug into that genealogy site online and their family trees never cross."

"If they aren't related, are they dating?"

Beth snorted. "Doubtful. From what I've found on social media, they like to have a good time and hang out with lots of different people who run in a similar social circle—if you catch my drift. They both have regular jobs. Hugo is a freelance writer for gossip magazines, and Pixie works at a spa and resort."

My head throbbed. "Do you think he's friends with this group to get dirt on their friends and write about them?"

She grinned. "That's my guess, which is why he would have been snooping in Andi's room to get the dirty details. It would be quite the scoop. Write an exposé from the scene of the crime."

"That makes sense. Pixie would be a good cover." I snapped my fingers. "I'll bet Shawn and Clark don't know what Hugo does for a living. They'd never want their lives to appear in print."

Hugo's cover is about to be blown. It's a safe assumption that his friends don't know the truth, especially since creeping into the victim's room would anger Shawn.

"Good sleuthing, Beth. I can't wait to add this to our murder board." I gave her a half-hearted high five, as tonight drained me.

"You haven't said—did you get attacked right away or did you have time to poke around first?"

How much time had I spent talking with Thomas Pennington's ghost? It wasn't more than ten minutes. "How long was I out there?"

"Almost a half hour."

"No wonder I was so cold. I looked around a bit, directly under the window. When I didn't find anything, I decided to look under the bushes. If I wanted to hide evidence, that's what I'd do and circle back for it later. It's possible that whoever went out the window had taken the coat and bag, stashed them there with the plan to retrieve them later, and hurried back into town to meet up with the group."

"Agreed." She slowed the car and turned into my parking area. "Oh, I texted my dad to let him know we were on our way."

Our families were waiting at the base of the stairs. "Whatever you do, stay with me tonight. We must get this new information on the board. In fact, can you run up the stairs first and hide it in the closet?"

"Good thinking. Dad, Dana, and Erma don't need to see what we were working on before we went to the inn. Dad will put one and one together and come up with the sofa sleuths investigating."

I handed her my house keys. "Which, Eddie's already on to us. We don't need three more people telling us to stay out of the case."

The passenger door opened, and Ethan extended his hand. I shot Beth a look that I hoped conveyed, *hurry*.

She pushed open her door and gave me a thumbs up. "Dad, I'm going to get the lights on."

"Good idea."

I took his hand and moved slowly—first to give Beth time and because my head hurt like the dickens. I smiled at Mom and Gram as they attempted to erase the worried looks they exchanged.

"Mom, Gram, relax. The doctor said I'm fine. My concussion was mild and other than a slight headache and a nasty bruise, no lasting damage."

"Except a scar. This is why you shouldn't be poking around a crime scene." Mom cupped my elbow as we climbed the stairs.

I glanced over my shoulder. The ghostly form of Thomas

Pennington stood on the edge of the property line, and he bowed his head.

Gram followed my gaze and cleared her throat. "The plot thickens?"

With a soft chuckle, I said, "Gram, you have no idea."

My cell pinged. With luck, it would be Eddie. I reached for it, and Mom said, "Can't that wait until you're sitting down? I don't want you to trip walking up the steps."

"Mom, I'm not a klutz."

"Under normal circumstances I would agree, but can you humor me for ten more minutes?"

I kissed her cheek. "Please, don't worry. I'm not going to break."

Gram said, "I'm making tea and serving pie, and then we can all get some rest."

We entered the apartment. Beth closed the closet door and with a sly wink at me, she said, "I'll take everyone's coats."

"Grandma, do you mind if we skip tea? You and Mom should head back to the inn and get some rest. It's been a very long day."

Mom's lips thinned. "I'm spending the night."

Beth said, "Dana, I'll stay with Claudia. She'll need your help tomorrow in the store, so a good night's rest is what she needs from you."

Ethan said, "I'll walk you over if that's what you want to do."

I shot a pleading look toward Gram. "Don't you agree?"

"Dana, your daughter has never liked to be fussed over, and as long as Beth agrees to call us if she has any concerns, I think going back to the inn is the right thing to do. We'll be over at nine to open the shop."

Behind Mom's back, I mouthed a silent thank you, and Gram winked at me. "Just one thing, Claudia, will you text me in a bit? I'd like to touch base before I call it a day."

Was that a code for who was that ghost we just saw? Or

had she chatted with Andi? Either way, I was going to call her in twenty minutes.

"Mom, I promise to check in with you both." I kissed their cheeks, said goodnight to Ethan, and waited until the door was closed before saying to Beth, "Now. About that murder board."

———

12

*B*eth pulled the board from the coat closet and set it up while I checked the text message—from Eddie, as I had suspected. "Guess who's checking on me? Your cousin." She laughed as I called Gram.

"Hello, Claudia. I knew you couldn't wait twenty minutes before you called me."

Her comforting smile was evident in her voice, and that hat instantly made me feel better. "Hi, Gram. I have questions, and hopefully you have answers."

"I'll do my best. But first, I must ask, how is your head? Not the answer you'd give your mother but the real one."

My fingers massaged my temple close to the bandage, wishing the ache away. I'd take pain relief later, but I wanted a clear head for discussing the clues. "I have a headache, and the numbing agent is wearing off from the sutures, but overall, I'm fine. I promise."

Beth tipped her head to the side and gave me a sympathy-filled smile.

"You wouldn't lie to your grandmother, would you?"

"Never have and never will." How was I going to ask her about the ghosts with Beth listening to the conversation?

"Is Beth in the room?"

"Of course, Beth's here. We're going to have cocoa and pie soon."

"Then I'll do most of the talking about our friendly ghosts —and yes, that's plural. I've bumped into the previous innkeeper to whom you spoke earlier—Thomas Pennington."

"I'm glad you are comfortable in your room. I'm sure the history is fascinating. Have you seen or heard anything from our suspects?" I hope she picked up that history referred to Thomas.

"Mr. Pennington seemed surprised that I could see him, but he didn't linger. It appeared he was on his way outside when I saw him. I'm guessing that was right before you met him."

"That sounds about right."

"I stayed with Dana and Ethan in the charming bar. Shawn was the only other person in the room. Where I sat, I had a view of him and the hallway. Andi drifted in and perched on a chair across from her brother. The poor soul. She tried to get her brother's attention, but he stared into the fire, holding a glass of whiskey."

"Were you able to speak with…" I glanced at Beth.

Gram said, "When Andi drifted out of the room, I excused myself to go to the powder room and followed her."

"That's a positive."

"Sadly, she doesn't remember much about what happened today, but she's felt sick the entire time they've been traveling. She thought it was something she ate, and just for additional information, they'd been traveling as a group for ten days."

"That would be an opportunity for a slow poisoning plan to be introduced. Did you learn anything else?"

She said, "When I was in the hall, Rhonda arrested Hugo West and marched him out the door. When I returned to the bar, Beth was there and said you would be right in. After about fifteen minutes, when you hadn't, she went out to look for you. That's when she discovered you out cold. I tried to find your ghostly innkeeper when I returned just now to see if, perchance, he saw anything, but he's not showing himself."

Beth pointed toward the kitchen, and I nodded.

"If he does you can ask, but he'd left before that." I kept my voice low so it wouldn't carry into the other room. Lola hopped up and curled into a shrimp shape next to me, and Herman followed her.

"He had? Darn. At this point, I'm at a dead end with information, but not to worry; I'm a light sleeper, so if anyone creeps down the hall, I'll hear them."

"Don't do anything rash, Gram. Whoever is trying to hide what they've done won't stop at stopping you."

"Don't worry about me, darling girl. Get some rest, and I'll be over early. Sweet dreams."

"Night." I ended the call and glanced at Beth in the kitchen before looking at Herman. Whispering, I said, "There's an innkeeper's ghost from the 1800s, and he keeps an eye on things. For the record, he can walk around the property but can't leave it. We might want to try that with you."

He nodded. "And there's a ghost of the murder victim?"

"Yes, all she remembers is the few days leading up to her death, but she doesn't know the details other than that she left her coat and bag in the entrance."

"It took a while to recall what had happened to me. That's not unusual under these circumstances."

The kettle whistled. "We're almost out of time."

He drifted across the room to perch on the window ledge. "I'll sit here, and are you positive that you feel up to working on the clues?"

I smiled at my ghostly uncle. Beth came in carrying a tray with mugs, a can of whipped cream, and plates of pie.

"I'm starving. Thanks for the cocoa and for staying over."

"Are you kidding? This is going to be a hoot. Talking clues, eating pie, and hanging out with my bestie. There's nothing better. Well, except if we had skipped the emergency room tonight. Any idea who hit you?"

"None. After I scouted around and didn't find anything, I wondered if a clue could have gotten pushed under the bushes when the troopers were investigating. Now that I say that out loud, if there had been any clues to find, they would have found them earlier. Anyway, I crawled around and worked my way to the backside of the shrub when I heard a voice say, 'Don't move.' In the moment, I thought it was Rhonda, but now I don't know whether it was male or female. I was reaching for what I'm sure was a buckle and tan fabric. When I looked up, everything went dark."

"Eddie didn't find anything hidden beneath the shrubs."

I pinched the bridge of my nose and squeezed my eyes shut, trying to remember any little detail. "I'm certain whoever put it there came back for it. If I had found it faster, we'd have the evidence, and I wouldn't have to wear bangs for the rest of my life."

She chuckled. "I don't think you'll have to resort to bangs. But if you do, we'll find the best hairstyle possible."

I grinned. "Should I consider it a badge of honor? A scar from our third investigation?"

With a wave of her hand, she said, "I don't want either of us to sport *that* kind of badge. So, can we skip attacks moving forward?"

We might end up in more precarious positions if we continued getting involved in crimes. However, I'd keep that to myself. "We should recap all we know so far."

Beth stood and picked up a red marker. "We don't have much to go on."

Scanning the board for what we had was disheartening. "Other than knowing that evidence was hidden after the area was searched, this means our culprit potentially had the items stashed in their room. But all the guest rooms were investigated."

She asked, "What about in their car; do you think the officers would have explored that option?"

"I'm not sure. It wouldn't have been legal without probable cause, right? But it's something Eddie could tell us. Let's focus on what we do know. The group walked to town. If they hadn't, that would be another option for stashing evidence." I sunk deeper into the cushions as my headache reminded me I needed some pain relief. Standing, I picked up the tray and took it to the kitchen.

Beth said, "I'll take care of the dishes."

"I'm getting some ibuprofen. Can I bring you anything? And before you tell me you'll get it, I'm capable—so sit down and mull over what we know. With some luck you might get a fresh idea."

I entered the bathroom, took the medicine bottle from the cabinet, and tossed back two. Stepping into the hall, I called to Beth. "Is it possible that someone laced her migraine medicine with a dose of poison?"

"Was it a prescription or over the counter?"

Herman said, "Claudia, if it were a tablet, it'd be hard to tamper with, but a capsule is another matter entirely."

I tapped out a text to Gram. *If you see Andi, ask her if her migraine pills are a prescription.*

Nothing like using all the tools or ghosts available to me.

"I'll ask Eddie. That might be a question he'll answer."

Jotting down this new idea on the board next to poison, she added *doctored pills?*

Discussing the sparse clues while filling out the murder board was the best way to end a difficult night, even though there was little to go on.

I checked my texts for the tenth time and finally heard from Eddie. "Guess who's stopping by just to see for himself that I'm fine?" I got comfy on the sofa again with Lola by my side.

Laughing, she tapped her chin and said, "Huh, I'm not sure. A certain cousin of mine?"

My cell vibrated with another incoming text from my grandmother. *Prescription.* It was helpful having her at the inn. Now, if Eddie wouldn't confirm the pills were prescription, I could tee it up so that he might say what they're not: tablets or capsules.

I didn't need to wait long. There was a quick tap on the door, and I called out, "It's open."

Eddie came around the corner and stopped short when he saw the board with our notes. "I see a conk on the head doesn't slow you down." He knelt in front of me, his brow wrinkled as he peered closely at the bandage. "A nice purple ring is making an appearance from under the gauze. How bad does it hurt?"

"A smidge. I took something to take the edge off."

He looked over his shoulder. "Beth, are you staying over to keep an eye on her just in case?"

"That's the plan. Also, we can talk about the clues we've uncovered."

He rocked back on his heels and shook his head as he stood. "Why can't you leave this to the professionals? Gigi being attacked should be a reminder that murderers have little regard for life."

"The attacker was trying to retrieve evidence hidden in the bushes. I'm sure of that." I kept an eagle eye on him, waiting for him to either disagree or flinch. Either way, I'd know if I was off base.

When he walked to the kitchen, he said, "Would you mind if I cut myself a slice of pie?"

"Help yourself. There's plenty."

This was Eddie's way of processing the events so far.

"Gigi, what made you think to look under the shrubs?"

He sat next to me with a large slice of mince pie. It wasn't my favorite, and he could eat all that was left as far as I was concerned.

As I ran my hands over Lola's soft fur, she purred, and I set her in my lap. "It seems like ages ago now, but Beth and I were watching from the attic window. You were about to go around the side of the building when I thought I saw someone lying on the ground near the shrubs."

Beth said, "I didn't see anything, but it appeared the area had been trampled over so we decided to run over and take a quick look. We didn't want to text or call you. If your phone wasn't on silent it might have alerted a perp that you were in the vicinity, putting you in harm's way."

The corners of his lips quirked up. "You were worried about me, but Claudia creeps in the shadows of the inn alone."

"Beth knew where I was, and the plan was for me to take a quick look. Unfortunately, it took longer than I thought to scour the area. And then, when I thought about what I would do if I had evidence—where would I hide it?"

He finished the last bite of the pie and set the plate on the table before giving me his full attention. "What specifically were you looking for?"

"The missing coat and handbag. We didn't see it downstairs or in the laundry or room four. When I stood in the door of Andi's room, I took a few pictures." As if it was my way to explain that I knew it wasn't there, I shrugged my shoulders.

He suppressed a smile. "Gigi, I knew you took pictures. I'm not encouraging you, but sometimes it's easier to give you a little so you don't take unnecessary chances. Like sneaking into her room via the open window."

"I'd never try to climb into any window higher than one story."

He chuckled. "That's good to know. Can I make a note,

that if you ever climb into a second-story window, I can remind you of this conversation?"

I grinned. "Sure, make all the notes you want. But can we get back to Andi and the method of poisoning?"

With a tip of his head, I continued. "She was taking medication for migraines. Was it a prescription? And, were they capsules or tablets?"

His eyes widened a fraction of an inch. "What makes you ask? And I'm not saying I'll answer the question."

That alone signified I was on the right track. "Hear me out." I shifted Lola off my lap, my mind spinning.

Herman said, "Be very specific with your questions. That's the best way to unearth the details."

"What if Andi hadn't been feeling well since the trip began, and she had a history of migraines? If she did, wouldn't she always have a prescription with her?"

Beth said, "I'd carry meds with me."

I nodded. "So, let's assume she did. Someone in the group didn't like her hanging around on this trip. We know from the argument Shawn had with his friends that they suggested it was better she wasn't with them, even though that was very insensitive considering the circumstances."

Eddie asked, "Then who tossed the room?"

"Whoever poisoned the pills. They were looking for the bottle. I'll bet Andi had one in her pocket and took it when she got back to the inn. For some reason, she decided to take Gram's skirt upstairs, which is why she had it with her. But later she came back downstairs before collapsing in the laundry room."

He frowned. "So, she takes the medicine, wraps the skirt around her neck, and collapses?"

"Partly. We're forgetting there was a water bottle in the room with her, but it wasn't laced with anything, right? Eddie, I'm sure the pills were tampered with in lower doses, and it finally caught up to her. She took too much migraine medicine, which caused an overdose of the poison."

"And the skirt? It wasn't tight enough to cut off her breathing."

I nodded. "Exactly. Whoever draped that around her neck was trying to divert attention. Just like in a cozy mystery book, it was a red herring. It means absolutely nothing."

13

"Gigi, everything is a clue," Eddie stated.

"No, it's information but not necessarily the right data that will lead you to the killer. This person is cold and cunning. Andi McGinty's death was planned far in advance; otherwise, it wouldn't have been a slow poisoning."

"We don't have facts to support that. Yet."

Beth said, "What about the headaches, stumbling at the top of the stairs? Claudia witnessed it. It's not a scenario anyone would want to think about, but is any murder?"

Eddie nodded, resigned to the facts we presented. "You're stating the victim's medication could have been tampered with, and she died from a build-up of poison?"

"Yes. It's logical." Now, I needed information from Andi to confirm my theory. If her ghost could recall any of these specifics and who hated her the most— I cringed at even thinking such a thought.

"What's the motive?" His gaze returned to the board.

"An imagined love triangle. Clark and Andi grew up together, and Ava knew it. Maybe Ava's spent years worried that Andi would break up her marriage and Clark would fall into Andi's arms again."

He arched a brow. "You know this because?"

Oops. I learned those details from a ghost. That wasn't about to be a confession I made. "I must have overheard them talking."

Beth said, "I did a bit of research while I was waiting for Claudia. Shawn and Andi's family is very wealthy, as is Clark's. Ava married into the Kline bank account. She was a pharmacy tech prior to her marriage. Pixie and Hugo aren't related. He writes for tabloid magazines, and she manages a spa resort close to New York City. Pixie and Ava's social media shows they've been friends for years. Long before Ava got married." She grinned. "I'm Beth-o-pedia."

His eyes grew wide. "You found all of this out while waiting for our patient?"

"I'm guessing your team hasn't discovered the details?"

"They've been busy taking care of the community, answering calls to the inn—like Hugo breaking into Andi's room."

"Did he say why he broke in? Was he looking for something specific?"

He shook his head and chuckled. "You ladies never give up. Even when I tell you I can't share the details, you keep pecking away at me."

I grinned. "I'd prefer you think of us slightly differently. It's like you're a sandcastle at the beach and we're the tide. We sneak up on you and, over a bit of time, wear you down to divulge what's inside."

"That sounds better than a bird pecking away at me." He sighed. "I can't confirm or deny sensitive information, but your theory is solid. And don't take this the wrong way since what you've shared could be vital to cracking the case but stay away from the inn and those people. If Claudia's correct, one of them is willing to murder one of their own slowly. There's no telling what they might do for self-preservation."

"For the record, I wasn't trying to get conked on the head, and if we hadn't seen something suspicious from the attic, we wouldn't have gone exploring."

"Ha. That's doubtful." He gave me a side-eye glance, but his lips tipped up.

There was a grain of truth to his statement. "When do you think the preliminary autopsy report will be available?"

"Soon. Don't look for me to share it with you."

I stifled a yawn. "Would you consider sharing what kind of poison was used?"

He narrowed his eyes. "Why?"

"I'd like to know if her death was as painless as possible."

He looked at the board and remained quiet for a very long minute, his lips pressed together in a slight grimace. When he started to speak, his voice lacked emotion. "Andi McGinty was born with a heart defect. One that she managed with medication and a careful diet. She didn't smoke, drink, or do drugs. By all accounts, other than her heart, she was squeaky clean. Shawn McGinty revealed that at her last cardiology check-up, she was stable."

With a snap of my fingers, I sat up. "That might be why she stumbled at the top of the stairs. She wasn't feeling well and maybe the migraine was a symptom of her heart issue."

Herman, who had been silent for a length of time, drifted toward me. "She could have had a heart attack and died. It wouldn't be totally unexpected."

That was an excellent point. "Andi didn't look like she had a heart attack and just died, did she?"

"Swollen lips..." Beth tapped the screen on her phone, "Aren't an indication of a heart attack. If they'd been blue, that would change the scenario."

Eddie nodded. "Are you ladies always so quick to look up information?"

I tipped my head. "It's a requirement for being in the sofa sleuth club. However, I think my brain is done absorbing new information. We'll continue stewing over the details tomorrow."

Herman remained perched next to me. "Claudia, you need to rest. The shop will be very busy tomorrow as it's the three S day: Shop Small Saturday."

Yawning again, I stood. "I'm sorry to be a downer, but I'm exhausted. Eddie, will you still swing by tomorrow and help me with the decorations? My family's coming over early to help me restock the store."

Beth said, "I'll bring new inventory over, too."

He said, "I'll help Beth and meet you at whatever time you say."

She said, "Eight would be good."

He walked to the door, and I trailed behind him. "Thanks for coming over."

Wrapping his arms around me he held me close. "My heart dropped from my chest when I saw you lying on the ground, unconscious and bleeding. It scares the bee-zee-bees out of me when you go off alone following a clue."

"I'm sorry I frightened you. If I had known someone was lurking, I wouldn't have been out there by myself." I stepped from his arms. "On the positive side, we discovered Hugo didn't stash the coat and bag. He was on his way to the police station during my incident."

"He could have had an accomplice retrieving those items."

I pursed my lips. "That doesn't track, and he's low on my list of suspects. His trade is gossip. For him to be inside that group? That's his bread and butter. There's no way he'd jeopardize a paycheck."

"You might be right. Time will tell."

Calling out, "Good night, Beth." He dropped a chaste kiss on my cheek. "Goodnight, Gigi; sleep well."

I locked the door and thought about everything that had occurred in such a short time. This morning, a young woman was alive, and now she was a ghost at the inn where my mom and grandmother were staying. Not to mention discovering the ghost of Thomas Pennington. I had so much to discuss with Herman.

Beth peeked around the corner into the hall. "Are you okay? I can fix you some Sleepytime tea with honey."

"Thanks; as soon as I slip under the blankets, I'll be sound asleep." Switching off the lights, I followed her down the hall. She was staying in Herman's former room.

He hovered in my bedroom door. I paused, "Beth, who do you think killed Andi?"

"Either Ava or Pixie. They're both in the mean girl camp. I still can't get over Pixie saying that Andi didn't belong in their group. And they, and Hugo, were missing before Andi died. I wish we knew why she went back to the inn. Was it for more headache medicine like she said, or did she agree to meet Pixie or Ava away from the others? It doesn't add up. Ava didn't come into my shop. Did she come here?"

"No. I would have remembered if she had."

"Exactly. Where did they go if not back to the inn?"

"We need the autopsy report and to chat with each of our suspects individually." I grimaced as I touched my head.

Her eyes drifted to my bandage. "The next time you want to check someplace out, we stay together. You might not be as lucky."

Beth was right. "Yeah, I got lucky tonight. Thanks again for staying over."

She smiled. "I'll check on you over the next few hours. So, don't get annoyed at me when I wake you up."

Giving her a lopsided grin, I said, "You can sleep. I'll set my alarm to go off every hour. Besides, we don't have that many hours left before the sun comes up. Your shop is going to be busy tomorrow."

"Which is a great problem to have on triple S."

I frowned. I had no idea what she was referring to. "What's that?"

"Shop Small Saturday. It's to drive business to local stores and not online retailers. Typically, I run a special on something. You might want to do the same."

Herman said, "Ten percent off gift cards is best."

With a smile, I nodded, "Thanks for the tip. Maybe I'll increase gift cards by ten percent with each purchase."

"How do you think of these ideas off the top of your head?"

I winked. "A ghost whispered in my ear."

Herman grumbled, "There you go again, taking credit for my ideas. She's never going to believe you're talking to an actual ghost."

"Now I know you got conked harder than you admitted." She bobbed her head toward the bedroom. "Rest. If you need me, I'm right across the hall."

I closed my door and perched on the edge of the bed. "Herman," I whispered.

"Yes?" He drifted to my dresser, and I was too tired to ask him to sit in a chair.

"There're a few things you need to know before we discuss the case. Remember, there's the ghost of Thomas Pennington, who sees most everything. Then, Andi's ghost is understandably a host of emotions. I can't get her to settle enough to tell me what she might have seen or the motive for why anyone would want to kill her."

"How does either of those ghosts affect me?"

I threw my hands up in the air. "Herman, talk to me about how I can communicate with a new ghost, and one who's over one hundred years old, to solve this case."

"Maybe they don't help you, but you can help them. The new ghost will want to cross over after the person responsible for her death is arrested. Before you say it, I know you're thinking I didn't. These are different circumstances. She has no reason to want to stay at the inn; it wasn't her home."

"That's true. I feel like I'm on a Ferris wheel of clues, going around in a circle with highs and lows but no clarity or time to examine each one."

"The poor girl died this morning. How do you expect to solve anything when you can't think straight?"

I flopped back onto the bed. "I don't know." In my mind's eye, I couldn't block out the image of Andi McGinty in Mariah's arms, with my grandmother's skirt around her neck. "What am I missing?"

"A good night's sleep. Things will look clearer in the morning, and if it helps, I'll go to the edge of the deck and call to Mr. Pennington. Maybe he'll be out and about, and we can discuss the case. Ghost to ghost."

Pushing myself to a half-sitting position, I asked, "You can do that?"

His transparent form shrugged. "I have no idea, but I can try." He zipped through the window, and I collapsed and closed my eyes, too tired to change into my pajamas.

"*C*laudia, wake up." A gentle shake and Beth's soothing voice brought me to the surface. I squinted my eyes. The room was bright.

"What?"

"You fell asleep with the lights on."

I sat up, looked around and noticed it was still dark outside. "I was tired?"

She laughed. "Undoubtedly. Can I help you get changed? You'll sleep better under the blankets."

"What time is it?"

"Almost five."

I got to my feet. "I'll get up. It's going to be a busy day, and a shower will clear my head."

She said, "I'll start coffee."

"Go back to bed. Just because I want to stew over what's happened doesn't mean both of us need to."

"Well, about that. I've been awake most of the night. We should head over to the inn and talk with Mariah before she's busy serving breakfast. I figure if we get there around seven, it won't seem overly aggressive to chat, and since we have shops to open, the timing would make sense."

Ooh, maybe I could bump into Andi's ghost. "That's a great idea. I wish I'd thought of it."

She laughed. "You can't be the super sleuth every time."

"Trust me, I have no illusions of being super at anything except as a seamstress. We might get lucky and bump into one of Andi's travel buddies, especially Ava and Pixie. What's your line of questions?"

"I want to know about Mariah's afternoon. Does she clean the rooms herself, or does she have help? Who was the last person in Andi's room, and was it a mess?"

"I'm sure Rhonda asked all the questions."

Beth nodded. "But it was right after Mariah found Andi. Now, she's had a night to sleep on it. Some details might have come to the surface while she was sleeping."

"You're assuming she slept." I selected brown slacks and a matching cropped jacket with a pale green silk blouse from my closet.

With a shake of her head, she frowned. "Think festive. You're greeting customers to purchase gifts. That outfit is lovely but consider wearing winter white slacks or even a long skirt, paired with a red or green sweater, and find a silk scarf to tie back your hair."

"I don't want to make the bandage stand out." I looked in the mirror and saw that the deep aubergine bruise had spread from the white edges of the bandage across my forehead.

"If you need help fixing your hair, just ask. You could use the scarf like a headband. It will cover the gauze and bruise. Maybe customers won't ask questions and realize they're engaging a stylish dress designer."

Herman drifted in. "When you're done chatting about fashion I have news."

14

$\mathcal{I}$ selected a deep green skirt with a coordinating cashmere sweater set in a lighter shade and a festive scarf in a rainbow of holiday colors. "How's this?"

"Perfect. I'll meet you in the kitchen." Beth closed the door and Herman lounged on the bed.

I dropped my voice. "What did you discover? Were you able to chat up Mr. Pennington?"

"I did, and he's a wealth of information. Do you know, when he died the inn was very prosperous? His wife remarried and continued to keep the establishment operational until their children were old enough to take over."

"That's nice to know but it doesn't help us."

He held up his translucent hand. "I'm developing a rapport with the ghost. Which is going to help us discover clues."

I sat on the bed. "You're right. I'm on edge, and my head hurts."

Herman sat up and attempted to pat my leg. "Thomas wanted me to tell you he's sorry you were attacked and wished he had lingered a little longer to have witnessed you being snuck up on. He's sure he could have alerted you, allowing time to defend yourself."

"That's very nice of him, and it would have been helpful." I rubbed my temples and took several deep, slow breaths. "He didn't see anyone loitering?"

"Sadly, no. He walked through the wall to get inside and hovered in the hall, listening to Beth and the others' conversation. There's not much to learn there since you have Beth's account."

I tipped my head to the side and looked at my friendly ghost. "How does that help us solve the crime?"

"He's spoken to Andi on several occasions. Thomas isn't keen on another ghost hanging around long term, so he's decided it's in his best interest to help us solve this and get Andi's ghost to cross over."

I half smiled. "If everyone gets something they want, I don't care how it gets done."

"That's the spirit." He grinned. "Pun intended."

Shaking my head, I said, "Cute. What did he say about Andi? I need specifics if I'm going to present new information to Eddie so he can bring the killer to justice."

"Andi has spent a great deal of time as a ghost lamenting that she can't drink coffee or chew gum. Apparently, those are her vices. But she's thrilled she doesn't have to take medication anymore since her heart stopped beating."

"That doesn't help narrow our focus, Herman."

"She remembers coming back to the inn, dropping her coat on a bench, and walking toward the laundry room feeling breathless and unsteady on her feet. This migraine was the worst it's ever been, she said."

"Do you remember how you felt when you had fallen to the floor?"

Herman drifted to the window. "You mean as I lay dying?"

"Yes." My voice was soft. I didn't want to cause Herman undue pain, and talking about his death was hard even if he had adjusted to it after a year.

"I was cold."

"Anything else." Reaching out my hand, it slipped through his translucent shoulder.

"I could hear Amos searching my desk, but gradually, even that faded."

That must have been as he slipped away.

He spun around. "After that, I seemed to be in the same room with Amos, and my physical body was on the ground. That's when I tried to talk to him, but he never answered me. It was then that I realized what had transpired. You know, the ghost thing."

"That must be how Andi felt, too." I picked up my clothes. "She doesn't remember taking another pill?"

"No. Is that important?"

My lips thinned. "I thought it might be." I went into the bathroom and closed the door, taking a quick shower, being careful not to get the bandage wet, then drying my hair, and dressing. It took several minutes to fold and tie the scarf to cover the bandage to my satisfaction. When I finished, I went out the opposite door into the kitchen, where a pot of coffee was gurgling and Beth sat at the table.

"How do I look?" I twirled in a slow three-sixty since any fast movement caused me to get light-headed.

"Fantastic, and the scarf is the perfect accessory. If someone didn't know about your unfortunate incident, they couldn't tell."

I whipped up a frittata and slid it into the oven. A hearty breakfast was the best way to start the day, but we needed to waste a little time before we went over to the inn.

Sitting down, I held the mug of coffee in my hands. "Beth, we're assuming Andi took medication when she returned to the inn. We agree it's probable she was slowly being poisoned, and it finally reached a lethal dose in her body. Maybe she didn't need to take another pill, she just succumbed."

"You're sticking to the idea it was slow and steady?"

"I am. Do you have any idea what time an autopsy result would be available to Eddie? Even though it's a Saturday?"

She wrinkled her nose. "I'll text Dad. He'll know the timeframe."

"Right. Former chiefs are in the loop on those details." I sipped my coffee while she texted Ethan.

Lola strolled into the room with a yowl and a head bump against my leg. I scooped her up. "Hello, little one."

She purred.

Herman drifted in. "When you see Andi, ask her if she remembers the water bottle. I'm sure it's being tested, but was it hers?"

I gave him a slight nod of acknowledgement. "We need to ask Mariah if the water bottle found on the floor was something Andi could have gotten from her room or if she'd have to have purchased it in town. I know I tried to see if Eddie would agree the water was fine, but he didn't bite at my subtle comment last night."

"You think the coat and bag are critical and that's why someone assaulted you."

"The bag, sure. The coat, maybe?"

The oven timer dinged. Beth said, "I'll get it."

The aroma of bacon and onions teased my senses, and my mouth watered. "That smells yummy."

"Thanks for making it." Her cell chimed, and she glanced at the screen. "Dad said Eddie should see a preliminary report this morning, maybe by nine."

"He's coming here at nine. I should call and tell him he doesn't need to stop over. I have everything under control."

With a short snort, she said, "That won't work. He'll swing by the station and then come here anyway. He said he was going to help you, and he keeps his word." She placed a plate in front of me, handed me a fork, and the bottle of hot sauce. "Enjoy."

My gaze drifted toward the whiteboard. "Any alternate ideas regarding the motive?"

Beth sat across from me, and her gaze rested on the board, too. "If it was a slow killing, it's premeditated, and from the conversation we overheard, at least Pixie and Ava didn't like Andi. You met her. Did you think she was insufferable?"

"For the five minutes when she bumped into my grandmother, no." I thought about my conversation with her after she had died and was confused by the new ghost thing, but she didn't seem unlikeable. "I'm going with jealousy, and we'll need to unearth why anyone would be jealous of her."

"Or, it could be revenge. But that seems unlikely. I've always thought people who wanted to get back at someone did it for huge deals, not a romance gone wrong."

I cocked a brow. "What if Pixie or Ava thought Andi was after their man?"

"Ava and Clark are married, but Pixie and Hugo aren't dating."

"To the latter, maybe not, but Ava could be insecure. Clark and Shawn are friends, and Andi is Shawn's sister. There could have been a romance at some time in the past, and Ava couldn't get beyond what was in the past." It's not like I could tell Beth that Andi told me the pair had dated.

Beth gave a thoughtful nod. "How can we find out the truth and learn if Ava killed Andi?"

For one, I was going to talk to Andi again since the information would need to be confirmed. I had to tread carefully. "We talk with Ava and Pixie. Together might be best; they'll be less guarded if they have the other's support, and we'll be the dynamic duo. It will seem more friendly and less of an interrogation."

"What if we don't bump into them when we go to the inn?"

"They can't leave town." I finished my breakfast and set the plate in the sink. "They'll need to do something to fill the day. Shopping might be at the top of their list. We also know they're not broken up over her death. I'm going to guess they'll be in our shops today, and whoever sees them first should text the other, and we'll have to drop what we're doing to get together." I chewed the corner of my lip. "It's not the best idea, but not the worst, either."

Setting her plate in the sink, she glanced at the clock. "Ten till seven. Ready?"

"Yes, and we'll just take the conversation as it comes. My main concern is that Mariah's feeling better today, and we'll coax out whatever else."

"You can start, and I'll follow your lead."

I knocked on the inn's kitchen door. Through the glass, I saw Mariah leaning against the counter, sipping coffee. Our eyes met, and she waved us inside.

"Claudia. Beth. This is a surprise." She gave us a half-hearted smile.

"Good morning, Mariah. Beth and I wanted to check on you and Oliver this morning to see how you're doing after yesterday's events."

She gestured to the coffee pot. "Join me?"

"Yes, that would be nice."

She took two mugs from the shelf above the coffee station and placed them on a small table. "Please, sit down." Taking the pot from the warmer, she filled the mugs and sat with us, sliding the cream pitcher and sugar bowl toward me.

"I still can't believe I found that poor woman dead." She shuddered, "Her body was cold—almost lead-like."

I placed my hand on her arm. "That must have been terrible."

"I was going to perform CPR, but I was afraid to try." She dropped her chin to her chest as her shoulders shook. "What kind of person am I to not try?"

Beth said, "Mariah, you're human. There was nothing you could have done. From what Eddie said, she had been dead for a while."

I nodded toward Beth. "Please don't berate yourself into thinking there was anything that could have saved her."

"Such a nice girl and so tidy. When I freshened her room yesterday, she even hung the towels up to dry. Most guests are lazy, but she respected the space as if it was her own home."

Andi drifted into the room and circled the perimeter until she hovered beside my chair. "Tell her that I was already gone when she found me. I watched her cradle me in her arms. It was the nicest thing anyone's done for me in a long time except for my brother."

That was a loaded statement, even if it was from a ghost.

I brushed away a tear that slipped down my cheek. "I'm sure if Andi were here and could speak for herself, she'd say your kindness meant the world to her, knowing she wasn't alone."

Mariah lifted her eyes to mine. "Do you believe that?"

I clasped her hand. "I do."

Andi's ghost attempted to wrap her arms around Mariah, but they slipped through. She cried "I hate this!" before zipping from the kitchen.

Glancing at the vanishing ghost, I pushed my chair back. "May I use the restroom?"

"Of course. There's one just off the living room."

"Thank you." I hurried after the ghost and discovered her perched on a bench at the base of the stairs.

"Andi?" When the ghost didn't look at me, I continued, "Why don't we go out to the porch?"

"Why not? I've got nothing better to do." She drifted beside me as I opened the door and stepped outside. "I heard about what happened to you last night." She leaned in close to my face. "You hid the bandage under the scarf. Well played."

"Thanks. It was Beth's idea. Did you see or hear anything last night?"

She whipped her head around. "Shush, Thomas is coming."

"That's all right. He's friendly."

She frowned. "So far, but ghosts are scary."

The innkeeper's ghost drifted down the porch, nodded in acknowledgment of us, and floated inside.

"He's fine."

"Well," her ghostly voice quivered, "I still think he's scary."

"Andi, I'd like to ask you some questions about Pixie and Ava."

"Those two leeches?"

"You didn't like them?" It seemed the sentiment had gone both ways.

"Ava is money-hungry, and I don't think she loves Clark. I tried to tell him that before they got engaged. Once she got her hooks into him, he believed every word that came out of that two-faced witch."

"Did Ava know that you didn't approve of their marriage?"

"Ha." Andi tossed up her hands. "Of course. I don't have any issue being honest, unlike some people. Shawn wouldn't utter one word either way. He kept saying it wasn't any of his business who Clark married. As his best friend, Shawn should have spoken up."

I tapped my chin. "Did Clark get upset with you?"

"No. He laughed everything off, said it was because we'd dated for two short months that I was jealous. I know that was a plant from Ava—it wasn't true. I love Clark—loved Clark—like another brother."

"What about Pixie?"

Andi's ghostly figure drifted in circles without speaking for what must have been a full minute. "Pixie's not one of us, and I don't mean that to sound like a snob, which I'm aware it does. She manages a luxury spa so she can blend with any crowd. She's been friends with Ava for a long time. I think that's how she met Clark, although I'm not certain. I could never figure out how they met. You might want to ask Hugo. Oh, and he's plugged into all the gossip. Literally. He writes it."

"You knew about him?"

She grinned. "Of course. That's how I got to plant tidbits about the hottest tickets in town for my charity benefits before we made it public. Hugo and I had an understanding, almost a friendship. Not that anyone knew it other than us. Besides, he was charming and funny. I enjoyed having him around."

"Andi, my last question might be difficult for you to answer, and I'd like you to think about it before you do." It was time to see if the ghost recalled someone giving her pills that might have been tainted.

"You don't need to sound so ominous. I'm already dead. There's nothing else that can happen to me. Well, except if—somehow—I get to stop being a ghost and find out what's in the afterlife. I'm hoping for puppies, rainbows, and never-ending books to read."

I pressed a hand to my fluttering stomach. It wasn't easy asking a ghost about who might have wanted her dead. "Out of the five people you've been traveling with over the last…"

"Ten days," she said. "We started with parties in Colorado with friends before Thanksgiving, then with family in New York City, and then we wanted some New England holiday cheer. So, we planned a road trip for another week, starting in Maine and heading to Cape Cod next."

"That's quite an adventure." I paused. "Who would have benefited most from your death, and how do you think they killed you?"

15

———

"**J**eez Claudia, when you phrase it like that, well, it's mean." Andi's ghostly form drifted down the length of the inn and back.

My brows knitted together. "Andi, I'm sorry. I wasn't trying to be insensitive to your situation, but I don't have a lot of time. I excused myself to go to the restroom, and I hope to see Ava and Pixie before I leave."

"They never get up before eight, and then it takes them forever to get ready for the day, but..." If a ghost could brighten, this one did. "I could see if there's a way to remind them about your store. They are shopaholics and have never missed a clothing store that I'm aware of. You could grill them when they come in. Do you have a business card or flyer to leave in the front hall? I'll cause a breeze and have it flutter to their feet."

"I should have one in my purse."

"Excellent. Not to worry; I was good at manipulating people when I was alive, and I'm sure I can do it as a ghost." She held up her ghostly hand. "That sounds awful. What I meant was I was excellent at convincing people to donate money to several charities I oversaw. As for who'd be happy I was dead, the girls didn't like me, and they didn't want me to come on the trip, but they wouldn't go to such lengths as to kill me."

"Then it could be any of them." I scuffed my boot on the porch.

"Shawn would never hurt me. We're very close; he's always looked out for me since we were kids. He's a terrific big brother."

"Now we're down to four." I heard Beth calling my name. "I've got to go inside but stick around. I'll get the card on the table before leaving."

I eased open the door and waved to Beth. She nodded, and I heard her say, "Mariah, she'll be right back."

Andi said, "Tell her you were admiring the painting above the fireplace."

I strode to the painting and took in a few details before race walking to the doorway of the kitchen.

"I'm sorry I was gone so long. The landscape painting above the living room fireplace caught my eye. It's wonderful. Has that always been here?"

Mariah smiled. "Yes, it has. In the late nineteenth century, the innkeeper, Thomas Pennington, passed away from pneumonia. After his wife remarried, her second husband was an artist. I can't recall his name off the top of my head, but he painted that picture of the bay."

"He did a spectacular job. I can almost feel the salty breeze and the sun's warmth on my face. It's as if I was there on the day he was painting."

She smiled. "From the stories passed down, Oliver's great-great-grandfather wasn't much for art; however, his wife was, and her new husband didn't know how to run an inn, so he spent his days painting. He made a modest living from selling his art, which helped support the Pennington family. At least they didn't lose the inn during those difficult times."

Thomas hovered in the corner with a scowl on his face.

"My wife needed someone to help run the inn, not drift around painting pretty pictures."

That poor ghost. "I wonder if the former Mrs. Pennington was happy with her new husband?"

"Oliver's mother found journals for the last three generations. Although Mary didn't journal daily, I suspect she had little time to do that. She states that her second husband was a kind man.

"Harrumph," Thomas muttered, but he didn't say anything more.

She stood. "I must get busy. An innkeeper's wife's chores are never done." She hugged us tight. "I'm feeling better since we talked." She smiled at Beth. "Thank you."

"My pleasure, and remember, if you think of anything out of the ordinary, you can let us know. We're *unofficially* looking into this matter," Beth said.

With a grin Mariah said, "Eddie doesn't mind?" With a quick glance at me, she smiled. "No, I'm sure he doesn't."

Andi hovered next to Thomas as I walked out the kitchen door. She pointed to the front hall, "Mariah, would you mind if I looked around the front entrance? I feel like I'm overlooking something that was there yesterday."

"Of course." She looked at her watch. "It's eight. Would you leave the front door unlocked since we're officially open now?"

Over my shoulder, I said, "Call if you need anything."

Once we were out of hearing range, I whispered to Beth, "Do you have a business card?"

She didn't ask why but withdrew her wallet from her coat pocket and handed me a card. I looked around and placed our cards face up on the table at the bottom of the stairs next to a short stack of the morning newspaper. I saw the question in her eyes.

"Good morning, ladies," Oliver said, as he descended the stairs.

"Good morning. Beth and I stopped by to check on Mariah and you."

"That's neighborly of you." His strained smile didn't warm his eyes. With a quick glance toward the kitchen door, he lowered his voice. "Mariah had nightmares all night. She kept waking up screaming *I can't save her*. All I could do was hold her while she cried." His shoulders sagged. "I wish I'd never gone into Portland so she wouldn't have been left alone to deal with the trauma."

Beth said, "Oliver, you had no way to know that would happen. Mariah's not angry with you."

"She blames herself."

I said, "When we were talking, she told us she should have done CPR and tried to save Andi. We reassured her there was nothing that could have been done at that point."

"You think the young woman was already," he lowered his voice again, "gone?"

A cold breeze brushed me. Andi said, "I didn't go anywhere. I'm stuck here."

"Based on the evidence, Andi McGinty was dead when Mariah found her. There was nothing anyone could have done." I hoped her ghost would understand my point.

He exhaled. "That's some relief. You told Mariah that, too?"

"Yes. I think hearing it helped a little."

Tipping his head to the side, he said, "Do you think she'll get annoyed if I hover today?"

I smiled. "I'd chance it if I were you."

His eyes locked on mine and then Beth's. "Ladies, if you don't mind, I'm going to hug my wife and remind her that today we'll decorate. That should put a smile on her face."

We stepped back so he could walk by. When he was at the kitchen door I nodded to Andi's ghost. "With a little bit of luck, the ladies will see our cards and be reminded they have nothing better to do than shop."

Andi said, "You can count on me."

Beth pushed open the door. "That's a great idea if they happen to look down."

Following her out, I nodded to the innkeeper's ghost, who said, "If the newbie can't get the job done, I will."

"Beth, have a little faith. I'm sure those two will be in our shops at some point today, and we'll have the opportunity to ask a few pointed questions. Our biggest challenge will be one of us breaking away from our store so we can question them together."

"Dad will be around all day until he and your mom go to Robins Pointe. You should ask your mom and grandmother to help you today. You can say you need the extra help due to your headache."

It wasn't a lie; my head was throbbing, and it wasn't even time to open yet. "I'm going to take some pain reliever before everyone arrives."

"We should take a few minutes to plan the questions we'll pose to Ava and Pixie."

We paused at the base of my stairs. "Come on up, and we can brainstorm for a minute."

"Great. I like knowing what you're thinking so I can bounce off you."

Once inside, Beth dropped her coat on the back of the sofa, and I hung mine up. "We've got a few minutes to iron out tough questions to make them sound casual before Eddie meets you at Knit or Purl, and then my family arrives at nine."

Beth said, "Correct. What's our first question?"

I paced in front of the windows that overlooked Cade Street. "Asking how they are after all that's happened. That question should reveal any true emotions they have about Andi's death."

"If they seem broken up, what's next?"

"How long have they been friends with Andi? Who might

have wanted to hurt her?" I snapped my fingers, "And would Shawn have any reason to want her out of the picture?"

"Wait. What? Her brother?"

Nodding, I said, "Whichever woman answers that question might reveal her guilt by throwing the grieving brother under the proverbial bus."

Beth's face scrunched up. "You think that helps us?"

"Yes. Think of it like this: we'll have to watch their facial expressions closely, even for a slight twitch. If either of the women blanches at the idea of Shawn, that could indicate they don't believe it's possible or they know who killed Andi. They could point their fingers in a different direction to deflect suspicion away from themselves."

"Claudia, could they realize what we're trying to do and come after us? Especially since you were caught outside almost finding evidence? They might be suspicious."

"We'll be extra careful." My mind raced with how this could spin out, but I had no real idea what would happen. There were so many holes in our clue board. I rubbed my forehead. "I've got nothing else right now."

"Me, either." Beth slipped her coat on. "I'm going over to my place, change for the day, and I'll be back with sweaters and more."

When the door closed, I called out, "Herman?"

"Here I am." My friendly ghost drifted into the room and asked, "What did you discover?"

"I talked with Andi's ghost. She'll help if she can by getting our business cards to flutter to the floor when Ava and Pixie are around. If I can get them into my shop or Beth's, we can question them without annoying Rhonda and the state police."

"That will be difficult for her as a new ghost. Moving objects takes time to master as a translucent being. I know from personal experience I still can't do it at will all the time."

"I forgot to mention—Thomas Pennington overheard us and offered to help if necessary."

He drifted around the room. "We must discuss you putting yourself in the line of danger again. This poor woman hasn't even been dead twenty-four hours, and you've already been clobbered over the head and received stitches for your effort of looking for a clue. I would prefer you didn't become like me."

"Oh, Herman. I love that you worry about me. I promise to be careful, and at least for today, I won't be alone. The shop will be busy; Eddie will help with decorations, and Mom and Gram will be in the shop."

He wagged a finger at me. "You have a knack for finding trouble."

"Eddie and you agree on that point. That's why he wants me to steer clear, but how can I? Talking to ghosts gives me a unique insight, and I'd like to help Andi cross over. She can't if her murder goes unsolved."

"Thomas mentioned he overheard someone talking about her heart condition. Couldn't it have given out?"

"It stopped beating, but not due to her medical history. Her lips weren't blue; they were swollen." I twirled around, rushed to the kitchen to grab my laptop, and plopped onto the sofa. "Herman, you're wicked smart."

"At least you're embracing the Maine vernacular." He perched beside me. "What did I say that put a stitch in your knickers?"

"Our killer thought her death would be attributed to her heart condition. They weren't expecting it to happen when everyone was together. A steady stream of poison in low doses would have pushed her to the edge of death while feeling unwell during the trip. I'll bet they expected her to make it through, but her migraines intensified, so she took more medication, thus exposing her to higher doses of the poison."

I tapped the screen. "The search I did was if poison could mimic heart failure, and it does—it changes heart rates and blood pressure, which in turn can cause shortness of breath and fatigue. I saw Andi stumble at the top of the stairs on her way to get more medicine. That has to be it."

"Now all you need is confirmation from Eddie as to her cause of death." Herman drifted to the front windows. "You best get downstairs. Eddie and Ethan just left the knitting shop with a handcart filled with plastic totes."

I closed the laptop and set it on the table. "Herman, thanks for giving me a heads up." I grabbed the aspirin bottle and flicked on the stairwell light before taking a deep breath. Eddie would know by looking at me that my brain was in hyper-drive, and it wouldn't have anything to do with shoppers.

I smiled after unlocking the front door and clicked on the soft overhead lights. "Hello, gentlemen. Is this everything I'll need for today?"

I took in the two carts stacked with plastic totes. It was a lot of inventory. "Is Shop Small Saturday that busy?"

Ethan took one handcart into the back room with Eddie behind him. "I'm not sure, but Beth's knitters have been busy and did a drop-off very early this morning. Instead of us putting it on shelves in her store, she thought it best to have it here."

"I can restock as needed. Did she catalog everything, or do I need to do that?"

Beth entered the store. "I was hoping Dana could handle that for us."

Ah ha. This was her plan to have people around just in case. "That's a great idea, and I'm sure Mom would love to help while Gram mingles with customers."

Eddie unloaded his cart and nodded to Ethan. "Can I borrow Claudia for a moment? I, um, need to talk to her about the decorations."

Ethan said, "Sure. Beth will supervise me. I'm hoping to confirm my plans with Dana for later today."

He didn't look at anyone while he stated his intent to whisk Mom out for the evening.

"Dad, what time are you thinking?"

"Three or four? We could drive up the coast and enjoy the view."

She glanced at me, and I nodded. "Ethan, Mom will love it."

"Great, I had a text that she'd be here at nine."

Eddie touched my hand. "Can we talk? Upstairs?"

He didn't want to talk about decorations, and we all knew it. "If this is about Andi McGinty, maybe you should tell me here since I'm going to give Beth the update as soon as you're done, and I suspect you've already shared the details with Ethan."

"Andy McGinty didn't die from doctored pills like we had originally thought. She died from a nicotine overdose."

16

───────

$\mathcal{M}$y mouth gaped. I looked at Beth; she seemed as gobsmacked as I was. "How does anyone ingest enough nicotine to overdose?"

"Nicotine poisoning is climbing due to e-cigarettes. We'll need to determine if she was abusing them. There was no evidence she was using nicotine patches, but she could have accidentally swallowed it, which would have absorbed into the intestines. The exposure was over a longer period. This wasn't a one-off overdose."

Beth asked, "How much would she have had to consume to reach a lethal limit?"

Eddie's face was grim. "Forty to sixty milligrams can be fatal depending on the victim's weight and current health."

"Andi was petite and had heart issues." I was talking more to myself than to the group.

Beth had her phone out, tapped the screen, and asked, "Claudia, did you notice anything specific about Andi when she spilled juice on Erma?"

"She was in a hurry and apologetic, offering to get the garment dry cleaned."

"No, her appearance."

Closing my eyes, I blocked out the mental image of her ghost and concentrated on the living person I had seen. "She was pale and out of breath, like she'd been running, and complained of a worsening headache. Remember, she stumbled on the stairs and held onto the banister for a few moments."

She looked up from her phone, her face grim. "Would you say that could have been weakness?"

"She was off balance, perhaps even dizzy; however, I didn't talk to her after that initial conversation." Would her ghost remember how she had been feeling early in the day? Another thread to tug. "Eddie, could her medication have been dipped in the same kind of liquid nicotine that's used in e-cigarettes?"

"They've been tested, and they're clean."

"Then how did she ingest the nicotine and at such a large quantity unless she was vaping? Was a device found in her room?"

He shook his head. "No, but we still haven't found her handbag or coat. It could have been stashed in a pocket."

Ethan said, "I hate to state the obvious, but it's getting late. Dana and Erma will be arriving soon, and Claudia, I'm sure you don't want them to know you're discussing the murder case with Eddie. It will only upset them."

I bobbed my head from side to side, hating to admit Ethan was right. "Once they arrive, Eddie and I can check on the decorations." I could've asked more questions, but a knock on the back door drew my attention. I hurried to open it. "Mom. Gram. You're early."

They each kissed a cheek. Mom's brows knit together as she studied the scarf covering my bandage. "That's pretty, but how bad does it look?"

"Mild discoloration from under the gauze, but it's not bad. I don't want customers asking questions, so Beth suggested the scarf."

"Do you have a headache?" Gram asked, cupping my cheek.

"A tiny one. Nothing to worry about. Would you both spend the day with me in case I need to step off the sales floor for a few minutes?"

Worry filled Mom's eyes. "Maybe you should spend the day resting. Erma and I can handle the store."

I took their coats and hung them on hooks inside the stairs leading to my apartment. "I'll be just fine. I'm going to brew a pot of coffee in case anyone would like a cup."

From her tote bag, Gram withdrew a white bakery bag. "Dana and I stopped at Brewed Bliss and got a dozen assorted muffins. Help yourself."

I took the bag and placed it on my worktable.

Gram waved me to the stairs. "You mentioned coffee. Go on, and I'll organize this, and we can have a snack before we get busy."

Beth pointed to the front door and gave me a meaningful glance. "I need to get back, but Claudia, call if you need anything."

"Count on it." I walked her to the door and dropped my voice. "Remember, text if anyone of interest stops in, and I'll be right over."

She nodded, "And I'll do the same. But we need to think of a question about the nicotine. Like, was she a former smoker trying to quit?"

"I'll be prepared."

"Claudia," Gram called to me.

"I need to go."

"Good luck," she said.

We would need a lot of luck to bump into my two main suspects. "Coming, Gram."

*E*ddie followed me upstairs and closed the door after him. "What are you and my cousin plotting? Don't waste your breath by denying it."

I widened my eyes and laughed softly. "You think you've got us figured out."

"Don't I?" He put his hands on my shoulders and looked me directly in the eyes. "Your safety is my primary concern."

My heart thumped in my chest. I felt like I was sinking under the spell of his blue-gray eyes. I swallowed hard. "I'm careful."

"You say that now, but we both know trouble has a way of finding you. Like with Amos, and just a couple of months ago your design client wasn't who they claimed to be."

"True, but it wasn't my fault, and I hadn't gone looking to capture criminals either time. I just fell into those situations."

"That's why I'm concerned. I like you, Gigi."

I gulped. That put me in the friend zone, for sure.

"That came out wrong. I don't like you."

My face fell. "I'm confused." The hurt in my voice caused him to wince.

"Gigi, once things return to normal and your family leaves, I'd like to take you on a date. It'll be just you and me. Luke and Beth aren't invited."

"You want to date me?" A flicker of hope clenched my heart.

"Yes. If you'd agree after I bungled the invitation, you'd make my day." Color rushed to his cheeks. "I probably shouldn't have said that."

"I liked it, and yes, I'd love to go out with you."

His face morphed into a huge smile, and he pulled me into a bear hug. "That's fantastic."

"Now, about everything else that's going on."

He looked at me. "Decorations or the case?"

"Decorations. Since I'm assuming there isn't much more to say about the case now?"

He pulled out a kitchen chair and sat. "She wasn't a smoker, present or former."

I slipped into the chair across from him. "How do you know that?"

"When we were in her room, her perfume lingered. It was a subtle floral aroma. In my experience, or we can call it my gut instinct, smokers' sense of smell and taste are dulled, so they go for stronger scents or more flavorful meals."

"I see. The pills weren't tampered with, so we need to find another method that someone could get it into her. The water bottle?"

"Just H20, except for some flavoring."

I cocked a brow. "Like lemons?"

"There were watermelon flavor enhancers in her room that she could have added to water." He pulled out his phone and showed me the picture after thumbing through his library of photos. "See, it's a clear liquid, and you just add a few squirts for a dash of flavor."

"Isn't the liquid used in vape pens flavored, which is concerning when it comes to children?"

"That's the stuff. Rhonda is executing a search warrant for the inn and the guest rooms. Whoever's the guilty party might still have it with them."

"What about Hugo? Was he released?"

Eddie frowned. "His credentials checked out, and he claimed he was poking around Andi's room trying to get a scoop for his latest assignment."

"That means he was traveling with them to get a story?"

Lifting his shoulder, he shrugged. "That's the name of the gossip game, I guess."

"And these people don't know he's a leech?" I pushed back my chair. "What if he's witnessed what's been happening to Andi and remained silent all for the sake of a scoop? Or worse, what if he was the one doing the deed to see how the group would react? That would be one heck of a story."

"I don't think it's Hugo. You don't kill your meal ticket."

I nodded. "True. Will you learn more from the autopsy report at some point today?"

"The medical examiner will determine the exact method of Andi's exposure to the toxin. However, the authorities will focus on gathering more evidence. What do you and Beth have up your sleeves today?"

"We're working in our stores." I tried to appear casual, but he pressed his fingertips into his eyes and laughed. "Right."

I wagged my finger at him. "We're not doing that again."

"What?"

"I say something, and you say, 'right.' I say something else, and you respond with, 'right.' It's a game you play to string me along, thinking I'll spill the beans. For the record, you did it the first time we met, and I caught on fast."

He grinned. "Just tell me the plan. Who knows? Maybe I can help."

"To be clear, we're not chasing any suspects today. We concluded that both women seem to be shoppers. We have two of the best boutiques in town. This morning, we left our business cards on the lobby table at the inn in hopes they'd find them and decide to stop by. When they do, we'll call each other, and when we're together ask casual but probing questions."

"You're hoping to trick them into divulging important details about the case while browsing in a dress or knitting shop?"

Crossing my arms over my midsection, I arched my brow indicating he was pushing an iceberg. "If we ask them how they're doing since Andi's death, they'll respond. We're savvy to tell whether its genuine or not."

"Is that the only question you plan on asking?" He leaned

forward so we were eye to eye. "One of them could be the killer."

"I'll see where the conversation takes us. There are a few additional questions I'm ready to ask."

"Such as…"

"Could Shawn have killed his sister and if yes, for what gain?" My tone was defiant, and I didn't care. Eddie needed to see this was a good plan.

He shook his head. "No. Just no."

"It could lead us in a different direction. One of them could say something about who they think it is. What if it's Hugo or Clark?"

"We know Ava, Hugo, and Pixie were gone for a half hour around the time Andi went back to the inn. But the three suspects being unaccounted for doesn't play into the murder. The victim had already ingested the nicotine. All that was left to do was wait until she expired."

I threw up my hands. "Which could have been sooner than the killer anticipated due to her body size and underlying health issues. What if they followed her to the inn because she was sicker? We're back to where this conversation started, and you have to agree that the police won't be able to unearth some of these details as easily as Beth and I can."

"Gigi, if you're determined to move forward with your plan, then for today, I'm going to stick to you like glue. They tried to deter you once. Killers get bolder when they feel they're running out of chances to get away scot-free."

A snake of worry slithered over me. I shook it off. "Are you trying to scare me?"

"Of course not. I'm trying to make you see reason."

I gave him a sidelong glance. Debating my options as to whether to send Eddie away or let him stick around; he didn't need to be my shadow—but I had to admit, it would be nice to see his handsome face all day.

"You can stay, but you have to look like you're working. Help carry bags to cars, restock shelves and racks, that kind of thing. You're going to be busy."

Herman drifted in and sat on the table. "This young man finally asked you on a date and now you're letting him spend the day in your haven. Things are progressing nicely."

Unable to respond, I smiled at Eddie. "We should pull the boxes down from the attic to decorate."

His slow, lazy smile captured my attention. "We can also observe the inn from that vantage point. We might see something interesting, too."

Glancing at my watch, I said, "You're right. If my source is correct, the men should be up and about, lingering over coffee, and the women will be making an appearance soon."

"Care to share who your source is?"

I cringed. Andi had shared the group's morning routine. There was no way to explain that. "Mariah must have mentioned something about what time they came down yesterday." I snapped my fingers. "Now I remember when Andi bumped into us, she mentioned she had to rejoin the guys. She would have said group if the ladies had been in the dining room." *That was a good save.*

"It's getting late. We should get those totes. We don't want to miss any shoppers."

I gave him a playful shove toward the attic access. "I hope you had a hearty breakfast. There are a lot of boxes up there."

He flexed his muscles, "I'm your man," and pulled the stairs down.

I hurried up first and went directly to the window that overlooked the inn. I wasn't going to pretend the view wasn't important.

He stood beside me. "Anything going on?"

"The window in room four is closed."

"We did that last night after the team was done collecting

evidence. Shawn's room is next to hers, and on the other side is Clark and Ava."

That was news. I never asked about who was in which rooms. "Are there connecting doors?"

"Between Andi's room and Shawn's but not the Kline's and Andi's. What are you thinking?"

"Who trashed Andi's room? I confirmed with Mariah that she had gone in, made the bed, tidied the bathroom and she mentioned there wasn't much to do since Andi had hung up her towels in the bath. Someone followed Andi back to the inn, used her key, and searched her room as she lay dying in the laundry room."

"Cold."

I grabbed his arm. "What if whoever knew she was dying wanted to find whatever they were using to poison her, to cover their tracks."

His smile faded. "That's entirely possible, which would mean there was a great deal of thought put into this plan, and they watched as she slowly died. They could have stopped it at any point but didn't."

My heart ached for a young woman who was despised so much. "Right."

17

———————

*E*ddie carried four boxes of holiday decorations from the attic to the living room. "I'll check the lights before I bring them down and then you can show me where you want me to string them."

Herman slipped into the room and peered into the boxes. "Drape them in the front windows on this floor, and the shop display windows for a start."

I pursed my lips and flipped open a lid to discover clear zipped bags with strands of white and colored lights. "I prefer white lights in my apartment windows, and we can try colored lights in the displays—but I've never been a huge fan."

"One string per bag." Herman drifted around to the other side.

"Herman was very organized." I picked through the next box filled with bulbs wrapped in tissue paper. "Are these handmade ornaments?"

He peered over my shoulder. "Of course. Some are antiques. Fiona used to keep her eye out for my collection."

"Claudia. Can you come to the shop, please?"

Eddie smiled. "Your grandmother's calling." He nodded to the bags. "I'll be down as soon as I finish checking them."

"Thank you." I stood, crossed to the wall mirror, and adjusted the scarf.

"You look beautiful. No one will know what you're hiding."

"You're sweet, but on the edge of the scarf—if you look close—you can see the discoloration." I had to wonder if I was targeting the wrong suspects. "When these women show up, I'll figure out which one is the master at deception."

"Your knack for seeing through people is getting better. I hope you haven't become jaded since moving to town."

I shrugged. "It's always been there. Sadly, it's been finely tuned since arriving. Dealing with the public is challenging."

As I reached the bottom of the stairs, I heard a murmur of voices. Rounding the corner, I saw Rhonda, in uniform, talking with Mom and Ethan. Her gaze fixed on me when I walked in.

Expressionless she said, "Good morning, Claudia. I'd like to ask you a few questions about last night." She glanced at my family. "Alone."

"We could go to my apartment or outside."

She nodded. "In the back."

"I'll get my coat."

Mom said, "You can wear mine."

Rhonda followed me through the work room. I glanced at the stairs, wishing I could let Eddie know I had company, but she was breathing down my neck. I snagged Mom's jacket and opened the door.

Rhonda closed and pushed on it to confirm it was shut tight. I was positive it wasn't to keep the cold air out but to avoid anyone overhearing our conversation.

"How's your head?"

I touched the scarf. "A couple of stitches and a minor headache. Nothing to worry about. Thank you for asking."

She scanned the area and seemed to be waiting for me to talk. I wasn't concerned with filling the void left by my answer, so I waited.

"Why were you outside last night? Beth came in, but you decided on a side trip?"

"I thought I saw something from my apartment, and the window of room 4 was still open."

"Why didn't Beth go with you?"

Crossing my fingers behind my back, I said, "You'd have to ask her."

"You saw Hugo searching room four?"

These short questions were absurd. "You know we did from my attic. That's why Eddie went to the inn. However, we didn't know who it was until later."

Her eyes narrowed, and I was sure she was longing to spout a sharp retort, but she exhaled instead. "When you reached the side of the building, what did you see and what made you think to look under the shrubs?"

"I studied the window for a while, trying to put myself in the person's shoes, the one who pushed out the screen."

She quirked a brow that spoke volumes, most of which I'd guess was annoyance. "And?"

"What were they trying to hide? Since there was nothing on the ground and I don't believe law enforcement found anything when they searched earlier, I decided to look closer. Then I started thinking about trick or treat."

"You're joking." She rested her hands on her belt and frowned.

"Not at all. When I was a kid, maybe twelve, I was trick or treating with a bunch of friends in the neighborhood. One of the boys had a pillowcase full of candy. He knew if he took it home, his parents wouldn't let him eat it all. My gosh, his teeth would fall out of his head. Anyway, he got the idea to get some plastic grocery store bags and put a bunch of candy in there, then he shoved them up inside the shrubs at his house. You couldn't even see the bags since he used the branches to camouflage them. He smuggled candy from those bags for weeks and nobody ever caught on. It was ingenious."

"How does that relate to this case?"

"Rhonda, think about it. If whatever was tossed out the window was too big to go in a pocket, the next best thing to do is hide it in the shrubs. They're big and bushy. The perfect hiding place."

She gave a thoughtful nod. "I'm not saying I like how your mind works, but thanks for filling in the gaps." With a half-turn, she stopped. "If you think of anything else, don't go off on your own. Let me know."

"Are you saying I've helped in your investigation?"

"No. I'm trying to keep you out of danger. I don't need another crime to solve on top of the murder and your assault."

She gave a brisk nod and strode to the alley, disappearing between Town Hall and my shop toward Cade Street.

Eddie came down the outside stairs. "I overheard your conversation. Why didn't you tell me about the trick-or-treat idea?"

"It wasn't important last night, and today we haven't talked about the case in depth other than my ideas for talking to you-know-who times two."

He grinned. "Only you can make a rhyme out of clues."

I slipped my arm through his. "On the bright side, she asked me to call her if I thought of anything else that might help the case."

Jerking his head back, he chuckled. "What? She considers you an asset?"

Laughing, I tugged his arm. "Not at all. Rhonda wants to keep me out of trouble and to quote her, she 'doesn't need another case to investigate.'"

"Huh," was all he said.

Once in the shop Gram said, "Are you ready to open? It's one minute before ten."

Rubbing my hands together, I grinned. The shelves, stacked with knitted wear, racks burst with outfits and holiday dresses, along with a small selection of Christmas stockings near the door were ready for the shoppers. "What are those?" I picked one up and turned it over. "They're lovely."

Mom said, "I discovered them in a box on the top shelf. Herman must have made them from fabric scraps."

Gram's eyes were bright, "He'd want you to sell these, too, and continue the tradition next year."

I spun around. Where was Herman?

She nodded. "Trust me."

Smiling, I turned over the OPEN sign and unlocked the door. I held up my hands and crossed my fingers. "Here's hoping for a great day."

Ethan said, "I need to get across the street to help Beth." He gave a pointed look to Eddie. "What's your plan for the day?"

"Stringing lights, moving boxes, and basically doing anything that needs to be done."

"You're staying here for the duration?"

Eddie looked at me. "Yes, there are a few loose ends Gigi's working on that I might be able to help with."

Ethan's eyes widened, and he gave a solemn nod. Did they have a way to communicate without words? Was that a cop thing?

"Have a good day, everyone." He winked at my mother, and it was sweet to watch her cheeks flush a deep shade of pink as her fingers fluttered goodbye.

"Claudia, let's talk about the lights," Eddie said, surveying the front windows. "Should I put them inside or outside?"

"Er, I'm not sure. We could check whether there are hooks and a plug outdoors."

"Good idea."

Herman drifted in. "Yes to both." He nodded to Erma before he slipped from the room.

What's wrong with him? "Eddie, did you see an extension cord in any of the boxes?"

"Sure did, it's red. Do you want me to get it?"

"Not right now." We stepped outside, and I had my back to the street while I studied the front windows. "If we line the full rectangle with lights on both windows. I'll add a wreath and battery-operated lights to the door. Maybe on the inside, I can use some of the ornaments we found to add sparkle."

"That would look great."

Herman's ghost drifted to the sidewalk. "Don't look to your left, but your suspects just came from the alleyway."

He was correct. In my peripheral vision, Ava and Pixie were chatting and looking right and then left as if deciding which direction to go. Holding my cell, I texted Beth.

Stand by!

"Ava, I don't want to wander aimlessly. Being stuck in this dinky town stinks."

"Who said anything about aimlessness? I suggested we should start at the second-hand shop, go to the knitting store, have lunch, and then go to the dress shop."

"I'm not trying on clothes after I've eaten a meal. My tummy will be round and everything I try on will look terrible. We're starting with Grants Gowns. This card says ready to wear and gifts." She waved my business card at Ava.

"Good point. Dresses, yarn, lunch, and then Twice Loved." Ava turned in my direction.

Behind her, I could see Beth standing at her door. When

Ava and Pixie started walking down Cade Street, she closed the door to her shop and crossed Main Street.

Everything was in motion. Eddie dropped his voice. "Showtime."

I smiled. "Good morning, ladies." I glanced at the bright blue sky. "It's a lovely morning."

"For some." Pixie pulled open the door, and Ava followed her inside.

Eddie said, "Tough crowd."

He held the door for me, and we walked in. Mom was in the back, and Gram asked them if they wanted to see something specific or browse.

Ava's face paled, and she pointed to a mannequin dressed in a skirt, frilly blouse, and vest. "Is that the skirt that was tied around Andi's neck?"

Swiftly, I reached her side. "No. This is a full plaid skirt."

Pixie said, "I hate pleats. Unless it's on a kilt and a handsome man is wearing it." She winked at me. "I swoon for a Scot."

Now that I had established her priorities, Beth walked in, crossing to the table of hat and scarf sets. Herman drifted by. Thankfully, he didn't speak. I wanted to stay focused on the two women.

"Ladies, I wanted to tell you that I'm very sorry about Andi."

Ava glanced at Pixie before saying, "It's sad, and I know the cops think someone killed her, but she wasn't a healthy person. She had something wrong with her heart, and over the last few weeks, she hasn't felt good."

"Yeah. Instead of coming on the trip, she should have gone to the doctor to find out what was wrong. With those headaches, her stomach upset, and she was so tired, it was a drag on the group having to change plans so that she could rest." She popped a piece of candy in her mouth. "Don't misunderstand me. I feel bad for Shawn—his only sister, dead…and so young. But if she didn't want to take care of herself, isn't that her issue? Now we'll need to attend her funeral and during the cheeriest time of year, too."

Beth said, "It's tragic. Do you think Shawn knew something was wrong with Andi and ignored it?"

Ava shook her head. "Are you kidding?" He was all over her, telling her to rest, drink plenty of water, and take her vitamins. He hated that she had a sugar addiction, which is why he got her that sugar-free cinnamon gum. She popped it like candy. I'd never say this to Shawn, but I think she was addicted to that gum. I tried a piece, but it was spicy, and I didn't like the taste. It reminded me of those red-hot cinnamon balls we had as kids. I prefer sour treats."

Beth nodded. "Chewing gum is a habit many people have. At least it was sugar free."

It was time to run down the rest of my questions. "Had you known her long?"

Ava said, "I've known her longer than Hugo. Clark and Shawn have been best friends forever; she was the kid sister who always hung around. For a while, she had a crush on Clark. He humored her by taking her out a few times. Eventually, she got the picture that he wasn't interested and backed off."

I felt Eddie tense behind me. This could be the motive we were looking for. "How long ago was that?"

She shrugged. "We've been married three years and together five. So, it was before we dated. You'd have to ask Clark for the details."

Pixie looked between me and Ava. "I met her when Ava and Clark got engaged, and we did a few things together for the wedding. But I wouldn't say we were friends. Except for this trip. Including her was important to Clark after Ava and I made plans to spend Thanksgiving together."

"What about Hugo? Pixie, are you two in a relationship?"

That wasn't the best way to discuss that hot topic, but they were being super chatty, so why not try?

She laughed. "Not in this lifetime. He had a crush on Andi and followed her around like a puppy dog. In fact, right now, he's back at the inn huddled up with Shawn, planning her memorial."

"Does Shawn know about Hugo?"

Pixie's eyes widened, and her mouth gaped open. "What do you think you know about Hugo?"

"Nothing." I looked at Eddie, hoping he would step in and help.

He cleared his throat. "What Claudia means is that Hugo had feelings for Andi, and did Shawn know?"

"He does now." Ava picked up a sweater. "I'm tired of talking about death and ready to shop." She handed Pixie the garment. "This would look cute on you."

The women turned away from us. Beth nodded toward the back. Eddie and I followed her. With a glance over my shoulder I noticed they had their heads together, looking at me.

18

___

I handed a customer a shopping bag, smiling. "Thank you, and stop in soon."

Eddie leaned against the workroom archway. "Can I speak with you?" His tone was ominous. Instantly, I was on alert.

"What's happened?"

He bobbed his head to the stairs. "Come with me."

I scanned the shop. Gram was helping a customer match sweaters and slacks, and Mom straightened the formal dress rack.

"Mom, I'll be right back. Will you cover the register?"

"Of course. Take your time."

When we reached the apartment, he closed the door. "I don't want this to go beyond us, at least for now."

"Is this about Andi McGinty?"

"Yes."

"Can I call Beth so she can hear this too?"

He shook his head. "I'm going to see Ethan next and fill her in, but I don't want your mother or grandmother to know."

My brows knit together. "Are they in danger?"

"No."

I stamped my foot. "I hate the one-word answers. If this is serious, but they're not in danger, why the secret?"

"Gigi, I want to keep them safe. The less they know, the better. If I could wipe your memory, I would. This information has shaken me to my core and it's baffling. I thought I had seen almost everything." He dropped his chin.

I took his hand. "Tell me."

"Chewing gum."

"Someone tampered with her gum?"

"Not exactly. We've concluded that someone switched her gum with pieces of nicotine gum. It looks like the candy-coated version we found in her suitcase. The sharp cinnamon flavor covers the taste."

"I'm confused." Dropping his hand, I walked around the table. "Wouldn't she have known she was chewing a different kind of gum?" Tipping my head from side to side as my neck cracked, easing the tension that lingered, I said, "Earlier today, Ava said Andi loved the spicy cinnamon flavor. I guess it makes sense. Was she a closet smoker trying to quit?"

"Rhonda double-checked with her brother. He confirmed she never smoked. Don't forget about her floral perfume."

I leaned against the kitchen counter. "Liquid for a vape pen has been ruled out, and her gum wasn't tampered with, just outright switched. Do they both come in a rectangular box?"

He held up his hand. "Here's a twist. Rhonda asked Shawn about the gum since we discovered a tin in her room, not a box."

"Let me guess. Andi took it out of the packaging and stored it in a cute tin."

"He didn't use the word cute, but yes, she kept a tin in her bag and one next to her bed, which she filled from the boxes she always had with her."

I walked around the table for a second time. "Then, how could someone have switched it if she was the one refilling the tin, and how much would she have to chew to ingest enough to make her sick?"

"Excellent question. Each piece of gum has four milligrams of nicotine. It was normal for her to chew two pieces at a time and for most of the day. The gum becomes flavorless within a half hour, and if she was drinking water while chewing, she was ingesting even more into her system."

"How is it possible she had no idea she wasn't chewing her normal gum?"

"She had no reason to be suspicious. Manufacturers tweak things in products all the time."

"But someone else was refilling her tin."

"Or were they replacing the contents after she had filled it?" He withdrew his cell and showed me a picture of a floral embossed round, silver container. "This was the one we found next to her bed. As you can see, it's decent size. It could easily hold a day's worth of gum."

"Eddie, are you saying that she filled it up, and someone dumped it out and replaced it with the nicotine gum without her knowing it?"

He nodded. "Do you remember yesterday morning? She told you she forgot her medicine upstairs?"

"And her gum. She must have kept a tin in her shoulder bag, which is why someone took it from the lobby."

"Exactly. We need to find the bag and coat. That tin may have fingerprints from the murderer."

"I'm more sure now than I was that it had been stuffed in the shrubs. I wish I'd thought of that sooner and gotten it before the killer."

"It could have been the killer's accomplice if two of them were working together."

"Ava and Pixie could be in on it together."

"Motive?"

"They didn't like her. Even though Ava and Clark are

married, I get the vibe she was jealous of Clark and Andi's relationship, past and present. Some women are very possessive."

"Okay, if Ava was jealous, why would Pixie get involved?"

I slumped into a chair. "Solidarity. Women are weird. I know if Beth needed my support, she'd have it without question."

"You're incapable of harming anyone. That's extreme. Even in Ava's situation, to systematically poison an ex-flame of your now-husband."

"I didn't say it was rational and mentioning that I'd have Beth's back in all situations is the truth. Wouldn't you have Luke's?"

"Not if he was trying to kill someone."

Drumming my fingertips on the tabletop, my mind raced. "We're missing a critical clue. We need to talk to the five of them."

Eddie gave me a stern look. "Now, *we* don't. The police do."

While I didn't like how he emphasized *we*, the implied warning laced his words. "Are the *police* going to search the inn again?"

"They're already moving into place. The state police are going to be on the scene with Rhonda."

I touched his arm. "Do you want to go over there?"

He shook his head. "No. I'm staying with you. You've had one encounter with the ladies today, and they might come back. Leaving you exposed to potential killers isn't something I can do in good conscience."

I nodded. "You're a cop to your core."

His eyes narrowed as confusion filled them. "Is that all you think this is after our conversation earlier?"

"You put the job first, don't you?"

He stared at his hands. "I'd never put my job before people I care about."

"Eddie, I'm sorry. I didn't mean to offend you. It's just that closing this case is important not just for Andi to get justice but for the Joneses, too. If word got out that there was a mysterious, unsolved death of a guest, this could hurt their business for the holiday season."

He looked at me. "I know. I trust that Rhonda and the others will conduct a thorough search. If there's something to find, they'll uncover it."

I slipped my arms around his waist and gave him a quick hug. "I hope you didn't think I was being a jerk. Thinking you'd leave to get in on the action is reasonable."

"I was that kind of guy before returning to Drakes Bay. I hope I've changed enough to be a better man."

"You *are* a good man. I'm glad you're in my life."

He smiled. "Me too. Now, let's talk about decorations and what I need to do for the rest of the day."

Giving him a playful push, I slipped from his arms. "We need more business cards from Beth's. Care to run across the street for me? I'll send a text to let her know you're coming."

"If you want to order lunch, I can pick it up while I'm out."

"I'll run over to Brewed Bliss and get lunch. We'll meet back here, in say," I glanced at my watch, "forty-five minutes?"

"Order me a turkey club with chips and a pickle. Extra mayo and a smear of spicy mustard?"

Giving him a saucy wink, I laughed, "What, no cookie?"

"Well, sure. Why not?" He stood, kissed my cheek, and said, "See you soon," and dashed down the inside stairs.

My fingertips skimmed my cheek where he kissed it, and a slight smile slipped over my lips. *I could fall for this guy in a big way.*

"Claudia," Mom called up. "Are you coming down shortly? Eddie mentioned we were ordering lunch."

"Be right there, Mom."

*P*ulling the collar of my jacket closer to my neck, I crossed Main Street on my way to Brewed Bliss. Traffic was brisk, and the sidewalks bustled with people carrying shopping bags. A small group of carolers strolled up the sidewalk dressed in costumes from the 1900s. I waited until they passed before I opened the café door and wandered inside. Business was brisk as usual. The to-go line was almost to the door, and patrons sat at tables enjoying a meal. I didn't recognize many people as I stood at the end of the queue. I had advanced a few spots when I saw Ava and Pixie at a table for two, which answered my first question about where the men were.

They hadn't noticed me. As I drew closer, I tipped my head in their direction, hoping to catch snippets of their conversation.

Ava said, "Do you think the cops will figure it out?"

"They're not incompetent; they've already uncovered how she died. I got a message from Hugo that they're searching the inn from top to bottom, but he didn't say what they're looking for."

Ava smirked. "Pix, if they'd tell us, we could point them in the wrong direction."

"You don't know what they'll find. What if they're smart enough to uncover the truth?"

"What truth? The one that says Andi was sick and didn't tell Shawn?"

Pixie scanned the room, and thankfully, she didn't recognize me. "Even if she had, would he have taken her seriously? With that heart condition, she never felt great."

"Hush. Someone might overhear us and think we had something to do with her death."

Frowning, Pixie said, "Didn't we?

Ava stacked their now-empty plates and cups. "I'm ready for more retail therapy. The second-hand shop is calling to me."

Pushing back, Pixie picked up the dishes and took them to the bussing station.

Then she waited for Ava to get her bags, who laughed, "There is one thing I'll miss about Andi: she always picked up the check."

"That's not an issue, Ava. You can afford it being married to Clark."

The line moved, and I took two steps. Had I just over-heard a conversation where Ava and Pixie were discussing how they had killed Andi? *I have to tell Eddie right away.* I moved up again, and there were three people ahead of me. Soon, I'd have lunch and be on my way back to my shop. I texted him.

I overheard A and P talking. They basically admitted they killed her.

I tapped send and received an almost immediate response. *DO NOT ENGAGE!*

Replying with a thumbs-up emoji, I put my phone in my coat pocket and moved one more place closer to the counter. Finally, it was my turn. My stomach churned by this time, and I wasn't sure I could eat. How could they just casually talk about this poor woman's death? What could Andi tell me about their relationship before I returned to the store? I needed to swing by the inn and talk to her ghost, which would be easy enough since I could go the long way back to my place.

Sue handed me a plastic bag with handles. "Good to see you, Claudia. I hope business is as brisk for you as it is here."

I smiled. "It's been steady. Thanks for lunch, Sue."

"Any time." She looked behind me. "Next."

Looping the handles over my arm, I hurried out the door and jogged across the street. Two police cars were at the curb. I skirted around the side of the building, hoping to sneak in the back door. Thomas Pennington floated through the closed window.

"Claudia, this is an unexpected pleasure."

I stepped back, startled at seeing the former innkeeper's ghost. "Thomas, I wasn't expecting to see you."

"It's refreshing to be able to speak with someone after so many years of isolation. I had the opportunity to speak with your grandmother as well. Charming woman. Do you think she would consider moving to our small town? It would be lovely to have more than one living person to converse with."

I didn't want to appear rude since Thomas had been helpful, but I didn't have much time to chat. "I'm sure Gram will visit often now that she's met you, too. Have you seen Andi today?"

"Of course, you'd want to talk with the *new* ghost. What's wrong with the old one? Has someone my age become irrelevant?"

"Thomas, it's not that. I'm trying to help solve Andi's murder so she can cross over. Isn't that what you want as well? You mentioned the inn wasn't big enough for two ghosts."

"Those weren't my exact words. But yes, I would prefer if she moved on." He drifted to the corner and turned. "Are you coming? She's currently curled up in the lounge, *moaning*." He shuddered. "An awful sound I might add."

Smothering a grin, I said, "I'm sure it's dreadful. Do you think you can keep people from the lounge while I speak with her?"

"Do you mean like assist you as a law enforcement partner might? I've watched the moving pictures on the screens in rooms. Many guests like to watch them, and it's been," he bopped his head from side to side, "educational."

"That is exactly what I need. Will you help me?"'

He zipped back to hover directly in front of me. "That will be quite simple. I've had decades to practice classic misdirection of sounds and objects seeming to move." He pressed a translucent finger to his mouth. "But if you tell anyone that I'm actually haunting the inn, I'll be very unhappy, and an unhappy ghost is never a friend."

"Are you trying to intimidate me? The one person who lives in Drakes Bay who can see and talk to you?"

He shrank in size. "When you put it like that, no. I'd liked for us to be friends."

His sadness vibrated the air. Who knew ghosts could do that, too? I had much to learn. "Thomas, we'll become very good friends, and you now have Herman that you can talk with. That has to be a bright spot in your existence."

"It is." He continued to stay in one spot. "Claudia, I'm sorry for trying to scare you into remaining silent."

I reached out my hand and held it close to what looked like his arm. "Thomas, I don't frighten easily. No harm done."

He whirled around and zipped the length of the building. "We need to hurry before law enforcement reaches the first floor. They've been working their way down from the attic, and the plan is to finish in the basement."

This ghost was in the loop on most everything happening. Hurrying after him, I asked, "Have they discovered anything yet?"

"It depends on what specifically you're hoping they found." He disappeared through the wall and poked his head out again. "The coast is clear, slip in the back, take a quick left —or wait, it might be a right—and Andi's lying on the floor near the fireplace. I'll stand guard."

He disappeared again. Would I ever get used to ghosts coming and going? I slowly turned the doorknob and eased open the back door to avoid its creak. Placing one foot in front of the other, I crept down the short hall, looking left. There was a room that I think Thomas called the lounge. Andi's ghost was face up on the floor. Her arms and legs were askew. If I didn't know she was a ghost I think she had just been murdered.

"Andi?" I whispered.

Icy fingers wrapped my arm and held on for dear life. "Why are you saying my sister's name?"

19

———

I whirled around. "Shawn." I wrenched my arm from his hand. "What are you doing?"

He glared at me and took a menacing step. "Why did you say my sister's name?"

Grief shrouded him. I couldn't say I was about to talk to her ghost; he'd think I was being cruel. Or could I?

Andi scrambled to her ghostly feet. "Shawn?" She drifted across the room and attempted to hug him.

"Claudia, he looks so sad. Help him. Tell him you can see my ghost. He believes they exist."

"I'm not sure what to say." This was more for Andi's benefit than for Shawn.

He collapsed onto the sofa, burying his face in his hands. "I didn't protect her. I hope she's in a better place. Running on the beach. She loved the ocean. That's why we stayed at this inn."

Andi sat on the other side of Shawn. Lying her head on his shoulder, she said, "I'm here with you."

Swallowing the lump in my throat, I sat on the table in front of him. "Shawn. I'd like to talk to you."

He lifted his face and looked into my eyes. "Andi said you were nice to her about the juice incident."

"It was an accident. No harm done." Jeez, that was lame. How did you tell someone his sister's ghost was sitting beside him? "I am very sorry for your loss. Andi seemed like a sweet girl."

He nodded. "She was often misunderstood, especially by Ava and Pixie. All she wanted was to be their friend. I wish I could have five more minutes with Andi to tell her all the things."

I clasped my hand over his. "Talk to me. I'm sure she'll hear you."

Tears streamed down his face. He looked at the ceiling. "Andi, I was proud of you. No matter how many times the doctors told you to live a quiet life, you rebelled. Showing everyone your physical heart wasn't going to slow you down. Your charity work—I'll keep it all running. I'm going to establish a foundation in your name and make sure that your work is carried on, from stray cats to clean water, reading programs across the country, and kids born with heart conditions like yours will get the care they need. I promise I'll make you proud."

"Tell him I love him."

"Shawn, Andi loves you very much, and she's thrilled to know you're carrying on her work."

His face morphed from sadness and grief to anger. "She should be here to do all the things she dreamt of. I demand to know who did this to her."

"The police will find out who's responsible, and they'll be held accountable."

"When? All they've done today is wander from room to room, talking to each other in muffled voices. When I ask a question, the female police officer keeps saying they'll give me an update when they have concrete evidence." He slammed his fist on the table.

I jumped up. "They're doing the best they can."

"It's not enough," he said, pacing the length of the room. "Clark wants us to go home and plan the funeral. How can I do that, knowing a person I thought was a friend killed my sister?"

"Shawn, who had access to your sister's room during the trip?"

He stared at me. "All of us. Andi never locked her room. We liked to stay at small inns without many guests like here. Just your mother and grandmother and the innkeepers. It was like that at our previous inn only that time I bought the place out. I didn't want Andi being exposed to germs. She hasn't been feeling well and promised she would see the doctor when we got home next week." His shoulders slumped. "She was being poisoned, wasn't she?"

"I'm afraid so."

Andi's ghost drifted around the room. "Claudia, someone did this to me deliberately? I didn't die from heart failure?"

I shook my head when Shawn turned away. "Did they slip something into her water bottle?"

"Shawn, I'm not sure. You'll need to ask Officer Perkins for details."

He said, "I'm sorry I grabbed you." When he turned, he seemed to have aged ten years in less than a minute.

Driven past logic I blurted out, "I talk to ghosts. Andi's in the room with us. She wants me to tell you," I looked at her, "say something only the two of you would know to confirm what I'm saying is the truth."

She smiled. "When I was five and had my tonsils out, I got out of bed to get a glass of strawberry milk, and he had a blanket and pillow outside my door in case I needed him in the middle of the night."

I relayed the story to him and watched as he grabbed the mantle to steady himself. "She wanted cookies, too. Ask her if she remembers what kind?"

With a twitter of a laugh, she said, "I didn't want cookies. Mom had snickerdoodles in the cookie jar, and they were Shawn's favorite, not mine. He got us strawberry milk, and a plate of those cookies, and we had a tea party in the moonlight in my room."

"She's here!" Tears spilled down his cheeks.

I nodded. "Yes. She has been here the entire time, and she wants to cross over as soon as the guilty person is arrested."

"Andi, do you know who did this to you? Who wanted to hurt you? Was someone threatening you?" His questions came out in rapid fire, and although I didn't need to relay the questions to her, it was gut-wrenching to watch him grasp for answers.

"Tell Shawn I received a note advising me to cancel the trip. There's a tear in the lining of my shoulder bag. I tucked it in there for safekeeping. If he finds that, he'll know by the handwriting who wanted me out of the picture. It hurts too much to say the D word." Andi's ghostly form faded from view.

"Wait. Don't go." I twirled around.

Thomas hovered in the door. "She needs space. I'll sit with her."

"Is she… gone?" Shawn asked.

"I think communicating with you about the past was difficult for her. She slipped away."

His voice trembled. "Do you think she crossed over?"

"Not yet. If you'd like, I can come back so that you can talk to her again to say goodbye when it's time."

He hung his head. "Thank you," and then he strode from the room.

Where's Andi's purse? Still holding the bag of sandwiches, I walked out the way I'd come. As I made my way back to the shop, I mulled over what I'd learned about a note and its location. The key to solving the crime was finding Andi's handbag.

Eddie stood in the back entrance as I walked through the parking area past my Jeep. His frown read like a grim head-line in a newspaper.

"Did you stop at the inn?" He took the bag from me.

"Yes, I wanted to see Shawn. I thought that since the place was peppered with police, I'd be safe."

"That was good thinking. How's he doing, other than awful."

"He plans to continue Andi's charity work in her honor. More interesting than my conversation with Shawn was what I overheard at Brewed Bliss: Ava and Pixie were having lunch."

He scowled.

"Wait a sec, I didn't talk with them. I stood in line, minding my own business. Can I help it that they were talking about Andi and I happened to hear what they said?"

"You didn't speak with them at all? Did they see you?"

"No to both questions. Now, let me finish so we can go inside and eat."

"I'm sorry. What did you hear, and should I call Rhonda and ask her to stop over?"

"You can decide what we do with the information after I fill you in. The women didn't like Andi, but she picked up the check whenever they allowed her to tag along. That's what they were going to miss, and those awful women laughed about it. Then, they mentioned that they knew she wasn't feeling well. That's when Ava said people were going to think they had a hand in Andi's death, and Pixie straight up said, 'Well, didn't we?'" I shook my head; a sour taste filled my mouth. "Can you imagine people being that callous? A young woman has been robbed of life, and they are talking about Andi buying their lunch."

"It takes all kinds of people to make up the world. This is good information, and I want to share it with Rhonda and the team. Did Shawn have any idea about the missing items?"

"Not where they might be, but he did say Andi had a slit in the bottom of her shoulder bag and often would slip important notes in there. Could someone have taken the bag looking for the tin or something else that she might have hidden?" I hated to lie to Eddie about how I came to know of the hiding spot, but it was for the best. Since Shawn believed in ghosts, he wouldn't reveal how we discovered this detail.

"Plausible." He tapped the screen of his phone and held it to his ear. "Rhonda. Eddie. Can you stop by Claudia's when you have a moment? She has some relevant information." He paused. "No, she wasn't searching for clues, but occasionally, a concerned citizen can see or hear something useful and, in turn, provide that information to the police."

He nodded. "I'll be here the rest of the day."

I waited until he put his cell away and asked, "Was she annoyed?"

With a grin, he said, "It's nothing. She'll get over it when you tell her what you uncovered."

"Is it enough for her to arrest Ava and Pixie?"

"No, but they can be brought in for questioning. Unfortunately, the hiding place in the shoulder bag is hearsay, and unless we can find the bag, that tidbit won't be useful."

"If only I had looked under those shrubs a few minutes sooner." Or if I hadn't talked to Thomas for as long. Wishing wouldn't change anything, and I needed to focus my energy on now and the clues I had.

"Let's go inside. I'm sure the ladies are wondering what's keeping us chatting in the cold." He opened the door, and I walked in.

Gram bustled into the workroom.

She smiled. "There you are. I'm famished. I had no idea working in a dress shop was so busy. I've sold a half dozen gift cards in addition to the pleated skirt and sweater sets, some slacks and blouses, and those hat and scarf sets are flying off the shelf."

"Gram, take a breath."

With a wave of her hand, she said, "No need. I'm having a ball. Thanks for asking me to pitch in today." She hustled into the salon, leaving me slack jawed.

"Was that my grandmother?"

Eddie laughed. "Someone's having fun."

"I had no idea she'd get such a kick out of working today." I unpacked the boxed lunches while Eddie removed drinks from the small refrigerator I kept near the desk.

"Ladies." I stuck my head into the front room. "Lunch is ready."

"Claudia, you eat, and then we'll switch. The shop's been so busy we shouldn't all abandon our posts."

"Mom. Gram. You eat first since you've been hard at work." I waved them in the back with Eddie. "I'll take care of everything."

Mom wrinkled her nose. "If you're sure."

"Positive."

Once Mom and Gram were in the back room, I straightened a mannequin in the window. I stared at the entrance to Lilith Park. What was going on between Hugo and Ava? He jabbed his finger close to her chest without touching, and she stamped her foot. I looked up and down the street to see where Pixie and Clark might be, but they weren't around.

Ava shook her head and took a step closer to Hugo. He held his ground.

"Eddie," I called over my shoulder, "check this out?"

He came up behind me. "What's going on?"

"Hugo and Ava are quarreling."

He glanced at the closed window. "You aren't eavesdropping?"

I crossed my arms over my stomach. "Too much traffic."

He laughed. "Always thinking ahead?"

I pursed my lips. "I'm trying to stay out of the fray as you requested, which is why you're my witness. Rhonda can't say I overstepped if I look out my window."

He covered his laugh. "What do you suppose they're fighting about?"

"Andi would be my best guess." I put my hand out. "Look. Here comes Pixie."

Leaning toward the window, he cracked it open and tipped his head closer to the gap. "We shouldn't let a good idea go to waste."

I knelt on the floor, crept closer to the window, and pressed a finger to my lips.

Hugo yelled, "What were you thinking? Telling everyone that you didn't want Andi to come on the trip. Now the girl's dead." He smacked his hand to his head. "She wanted you to like her. All she wanted was to be your friend."

Ava shouted, "She dated Clark. That bugged me. How would you feel if she dated your husband?"

"Well, I'm not married, and I wanted to have a future with Andi. That won't happen now, and it's your fault!" He stormed through the gates of the park."

Pixie slid her arm around Ava's waist. They tipped their heads together. I could see their mouths move, but they weren't talking loud enough to hear what was said.

Eddie closed the window. "I'm going after Hugo."

I stood up. "Me too."

"Stay here."

Ava and Pixie rushed after him.

"If Hugo knows Ava killed Andi, he could be a target for revenge. With Pixie and her together, who knows what they'll do."

"Eddie, I can help."

"You need to tell Rhonda everything that's happened. It's too much to send a text."

"All right." I didn't want to agree, but he was right. Rhonda needed to be brought up to speed, and someone had to follow Hugo to make sure he didn't become another ghost. "At least ask Ethan to meet you."

"No time for that. Don't worry; this is my job." With a kiss on my cheek, he rushed into the back and returned wearing his coat and then jogged out the front door.

He crossed the street and disappeared through the park's gate.

I ran into the back. "Can you keep on eye on the shop? I need to find Rhonda. She's at the inn and Eddie might be in trouble."

Mom's face paled. "Yes. Hurry."

Gram called after me. "Be careful, and if you need help, call for Thomas."

I heard Mom ask, "Who's Thomas?" as the door closed.

I ran down the alley and came out on Main Street. The front door would be best since the police cars were in the back. I hoped Thomas would tell me where everyone was inside before I searched for Rhonda.

I rounded the corner and stepped on the doorstep. My hand hovered over the doorknob when someone touched my shoulder. "Clark!"

20

———

"Claudia, I didn't mean to startle you, but you need to come with me right away. I've discovered something important, and it could be a critical clue regarding Andi's death. Time is of the essence."

Who said that anymore? That line was right out of an old movie. However, I was curious. "Why not just turn over what you found to the police?"

He reached around me and pushed open the door shoving me inside as he looked over his shoulder. "We have to get inside before *she* comes back."

I didn't miss the emphasis he put on *she*. "Who are you referring to?"

He closed the door and flipped the deadbolt into place. "Pixie."

"We should leave the door unlocked. It's a main entrance. Fire codes and all. You wouldn't want to get Oliver in trouble with the fire marshal, would you?"

"We won't be long." He took my arm and guided me down the hall into the side parlor, which was set apart from the main entrance. Foot traffic would be non-existent.

At least he didn't close that door. Stammering a bit, I said,

"I- I should go. I only ran over to get something for my grandmother. She'll be worried if I don't get back soon." I slid a half a foot toward the door.

"Your grandmother can wait. This is a matter of arresting Andi's killer." He focused on me. "This won't take long if you'd just be quiet."

Sliding my clammy hands over my skirt, I nodded. "Go ahead. I'm listening."

"You have to promise that what I'm about to reveal is something you'll take seriously and go straight to the cops. I overheard Pixie trying to charm Hugo into leaving town today, and if they do, she'll become a ghost."

It's ironic there were three ghosts in my life right now. But he was speaking metaphorically, not about real ghosts. Without moving, I scanned the room. Too bad one of the resident ghosts didn't follow us in here; I could use some backup. Not that I thought Clark would hurt me, since he was bent on proving that Pixie harmed his friend. But there was a wildness to his eyes that made me want to disappear.

"What did you want to show me, Clark?"

He licked his lips and looked around.

"We're alone," I encouraged.

He handed me two folded slips of paper. Instead of taking them I asked, "Can you put them on the table and unfold them. I don't want to touch them and get my fingerprints on them."

"Good thinking." Not that he was wearing gloves, but I guess he didn't care if his prints were on the pages.

He tapped the one on my left. "I found this in my shaving kit and the other is a note Pixie slipped under our door this morning for Ava."

A, You shouldn't have come on this trip. I warned you. Now, you'll pay the consequence.

The second said,

A, I'm in the dining room. Meet me for breakfast. Can't wait for this trip to end. P

He said, "Pixie wrote both notes."

I leaned closer and noticed the loop to the capital letters A and I and the word *trip* was identical. If these notes were authentic, Pixie had sent Andi the first note. But how did it get in Clark's shaving kit?

"Both notes were in your room? How would the first one have gotten there if it was sent to Andi?"

Thomas Pennington's ghost drifted in. "Claudia, what are you doing in this room with that man?"

Sadly, I couldn't answer him. I turned my head from Clark and mouthed the words, *get help*, to Thomas.

He zipped from the room, and I had no idea how he might accomplish the task, but he had over one hundred and fifty years of ghost hijinks under his translucent belt. Where was Andi? She could confirm if this were the note she had hidden and if it was Pixie's handwriting, but so far she was keeping her distance.

"I have no idea how the first note, threatening that poor sick girl, ended up in my room but it did. What are you going to do about it?"

"Clark, you need to call the police and turn these documents over to them right away. Pixie, Ava, and Hugo are in the park."

"Is Shawn with them?"

"No." My brow furrowed. That was an odd question. "I'm assuming he's here, possibly in his room."

He clenched his fist to his side. Mumbling to himself, he said, "Now, what do I do?"

"I'll call the police." I withdrew my cell, and he wrenched it from my hand.

"No. I'll do the calling when it's time, not you."

My throat constricted, and I had difficulty swallowing. "Clark?"

He whirled around and advanced on me. "Keep quiet. I have to think."

"Maybe I can help?" I clasped my trembling hands together.

"You have. Pointing out the hole in my claim was enough."

"Clark, did you kill Andi?" My stomach dropped. I had never regarded Clark as a real suspect; even Shawn seemed more viable.

Anger vibrated in his voice. "No, I didn't kill her. She did that to herself with that stupid gum habit. She was only supposed to get sick!"

I lowered my voice to a whisper and blinked rapidly. "What did you do to Andi?"

"Where's Ava? She can fix this." He patted his pockets, I guessed looking for his phone.

Should I offer him the chance to use mine? Or could that tip her off? I knew what had happened, but I needed more information.

"Clark, talk to me. Maybe we can fix this."

He threw up his hands. "Ava has always been jealous of my friendship with Andi. She thought Andi was prettier than her and said I had made a mistake marrying her and not making it work with Andi." He sunk to a chair. "Ava never understood. Andi and I have been great friends from the time we were kids. I thought if Andi got sick, she'd stay home, and for once, Ava would see that she came first."

"You're saying you switched her gum with the nicotine version?"

"Yes," he murmured. "How was I to know that she'd chew that much gum in a day? Besides, if she had just stayed home, none of this would have happened."

Andi breezed into the room. "Did Clark just say he's responsible for my current state?" The translucent form of Andi's ghost undulated as her words grew louder. "Claudia?"

"Clark, you're blaming Andi for chewing too many pieces of gum in a day? That's over the top, don't you think?"

He hung his head. "All my wife wanted was a vacation without Andi. Every time our group went away, she came. Ava struggled to get over the fact that we dated. Even though the romance never blossomed. Do you blame me for wishing she'd get sick and just stay home? Just this one time?"

"That's the most selfish excuse I've heard." I circled the room, trying to figure out how I could get him to confess to the authorities. "Did you realize that with her heart condition, nicotine gum could be dangerous? It affects blood pressure and causes headaches. It might have interacted with her medication. I'm going to see if I can find Rhonda. You can tell her what happened—that it was a mistake—and you never meant for Andi to die."

"It was an accident." He lunged for my arm.

I jumped back before his fingers latched onto me. "Hey, what are you doing?"

"Stopping you. I'm not going to turn myself in. I'll take these notes to the police like you suggested and point the guilty finger at Pixie. She could have easily snuck into Andi's room and changed out the gum."

"Clark, that's not right." Andi's ghost drifted closer to him. "Claudia, what kind of person would try and frame another?"

He reached for me again. This time, I wasn't fast enough to get away. "You're not going to say a word."

I tried to wrench my arm away without success. "Ow, Clark. You're hurting me."

"Come with me." He steered me out of the room and toward a set of stairs in the back.

"Where are we going?"

"I'm going to lock you in Andi's room. They'll never think of looking for you there. Then, I'm going to find my wife, and we're leaving town."

As Cleark was half dragging me up the steps, I cried out again as I stumbled and hit my shin. He slid his arm around my waist and half carried me the rest of the way. Looking down the hallway to the right then left, he said, "Move."

When we reached the door to room four, he unlocked it and shoved me under the crime scene tape, shut the door, and flipped the lock. He dragged the desk chair into a corner and said, "Sit down. If you're quiet, I won't hurt you."

"Did you search this room?" It was now or maybe never, and I needed answers.

"Of course. I was searching for the blasted tins Andi kept her gum in without success." His cold eyes caused a shiver to race down my back. "It was helpful in switching out the gum."

"And you're the one who attacked me outside?"

"When I saw you from the window searching around the bushes, I knew it was a matter of time until you found her coat and bag. I had to stop you." He pointed to my scarf. "Give me that."

"No. I won't."

Withdrawing a bandana from his jacket pocket, he shook it out and tied my wrists together.

"Hey, you're cutting off my circulation."

He glanced up. "At least you have blood to circulate."

Thomas's ghostly form appeared from the door. He rushed to my side. "Don't let him tie you up. You must move. Those officials aren't taking the hint something's wrong. I need you to get to the hall and yell."

"Why did you lock the door?" If I kept him talking, would it slow him down from harming me?

He pulled the scarf from my head, and I winced as it caught on the edge of the bandage. I cried out and he reached for a belt on the floor. Andi whooshed into the room and ran her ghostly form through his. "Claudia, run!"

I leapt to my feet and stumbled over a pile of clothes as I reached the door and turned the lock, wrenching open the door. Clark was behind me forcing me against the sturdy wood.

He grabbed my shoulder and whirled me back into the room. As the door shut, I screamed. "HELP!"

"I'm not going to hurt you. Just buying a little time to get out of town." He tipped his head.

Footsteps pounded up the stairs and stopped. I heard Eddie's voice, "Claudia!"

"FOUR!"

Thomas faded through the door.

"Don't go," I cried.

Andi hovered close. "He's getting help."

Clark looked between the door and the window. He dragged me across the room and threw up the sash.

"What are you going to do now?"

"We're leaving. Jump or I toss you out."

"No." My voice quivered, but I didn't shed a tear from the fear that had wrapped its cold, ice-like fingers around my heart. "I'm not going anywhere with you."

He had one leg out the window and his hand on the cloth that bound my wrists. I thrust my hands to the floor and broke his grip. I said, "Think about what you're doing. Come with me to the police. You can explain everything—but becoming a fugitive with a hostage is not in your best interest."

His over-bright eyes met mine. "I've gone too far. There's no hope."

"That's where you're wrong. The officers with the local

police department are reasonable. If you tell them what happened and turn over Andi's handbag and coat and explain it was an accident, all that will be entered into the official record."

"Shawn will never forgive me." He dropped his head for a moment before a crash in the hall drew his attention again. He reached for me but got nothing but air.

The door opened, and Eddie burst in, handgun drawn with Rhonda behind him. He yelled. "FREEZE!"

Clark leaned out the window, ready to leap. From below, I heard, "It's over, Kline."

Eddie rushed forward and pulled me away from Clark. He wrapped his arms around me. "Are you all right?" He untied the handkerchief rubbing the skin where it was white from the tight binds.

I nodded. "Yes. Clark switched the gum. He was going to frame Pixie and leave town with Ava."

Eddie nodded to Rhonda. "Arrest him for the death of Andi McGinty, and the assault and unlawful detainment of Claudia Grant."

Thomas floated in the door. "Claudia, you're safe now?"

I nodded to him. Andi's ghost said, "Claudia, something is happening. I feel different. Can we find Shawn, and fast?"

Now that Clark was under arrest, did that mean Andi would leave this existence? "Eddie, I need to talk to Shawn for a minute. Can I give a statement after?"

His brow arched. "You're not going to inform him about Clark, are you?"

I shook my head. "No. But I'm sure after you do, he'll want to leave right away—and I'd like to pay my respects one last time."

He kissed the top of my head, and picked up my scarf, handing it to me. I gave him a small smile of thanks.

"I'll wait for you downstairs."

I felt his eyes on me as I stepped into the hall. Shawn was at the end, watching Rhonda take Clark from the room in handcuffs.

"Is it over?" he asked, his voice thick with grief.

"It is. Can we talk in your room for a moment?"

Andi's ghost floated next to me as Shawn opened his door, and we went inside. She drifted next to her brother, her hand hovering over his heart.

"Shawn, your sister's here."

His eyes rimmed with tears. "Andi, if you can hear me, I'm so sorry I didn't protect you from those vile people."

"I don't blame you, Shawn. I should have told you Clark asked me to stay home after you said I was coming on this trip. We always have so much fun traveling, and I didn't want to miss Thanksgiving with you."

I repeated what she said.

Tears slid down his cheeks. "I wish you had. There was never a doubt I would have stayed with you."

"Claudia, ask him to open his arms."

"Shawn, Andi's asked that you open your arms so she can be wrapped in them one last time." A sob caught in my chest.

He did as I asked, and Andi pressed her translucent body close to his. "Now, wrap your arms around her as if she were still here."

"Shawn, I'll watch over you wherever I go. Remember this moment. You were the best big brother a girl could have." She placed her ghostly hand on his cheek as she faded.

"I love you, Andi."

When her ghost was gone, I wrapped my arms around Shawn. "She's going to be fine, now."

He held me tight. "Thank you for everything. You made a very difficult part of my life a tad more bearable. Especially since I had these precious moments with Andi."

"I'm very sorry for your loss."

When I left the room, I leaned against the wall and closed my eyes. I felt a cool breeze on my face.

Thomas's voice whispered in my ear. "That was the most beautiful gift you could have given to that brokenhearted man."

"Thank you, Thomas. I'm not sure I want to do that again." I took several deep breaths and straightened up.

My new friendly ghost hovered, his face scrunched up.

"Were you worried about me?"

"Of course. I didn't want you to become a ghost, too. This inn isn't big enough for more than one." With that he floated down the hall and through a wall.

There was just one unanswered question: why did Andi have the skirt tied around her neck? I guess I'd never know, now.

*than opened the door to his house and pulled me inside with a fatherly hug. "Welcome to Sunday night dinner. Come in, it's freezing out."

"Am I the last to arrive?" The aroma of basil and oregano drifted toward me. Mom was cooking. I smiled. What was it about your mother's home cooking that could instantly bring you back to childhood?

"Yes. Beth and Luke are in the kitchen with Dana; Eddie is throwing a couple of logs on the fire. But now that you're here, the party can really get started."

"And my grandmother and Fiona?"

"Erma's opening the wine, and I believe Fiona is slicing the focaccia." He took my jacket, scarf, and hat. "How's the head?"

"It's fine." Tonight, I hadn't bothered to cover the bandage. I was surrounded by friends and family—it didn't matter that the purple had spread around my eye and up to my hairline.

We entered the spacious kitchen. The table was set for eight people. I kissed my mom's and grandmother's cheeks. "Hey, everyone. Sorry I'm running a little behind. I needed to stop home and take care of a couple of things after the lighting ceremony." I didn't say Herman had wanted to go over everything that happened the day before for the fifth time. He had been curious about Andi's departure the most and continued to ask questions that I didn't have answers to.

Mom handed me a slice of bread topped with mozzarella, bruschetta, and a drizzle of balsamic vinegar and Gram handed me a glass of red wine.

"Catch up," she said.

Eddie pulled out a stool. "You might as well sit and fill everyone in on the details of the case before dinner. Since officially I can't talk about it."

Mom sprinkled chiffonade basil leaves into her sauce. "How did you figure everything out about Clark, and how do Hugo, Pixie, and Ava figure into the plot to keep Andi from vacationing with them?"

"Hugo was in love with Andi so he was furious with the girls for wanting Andi to stay home. To be honest, I didn't figure it out until Clark started rambling. I was convinced it was Pixie and Ava who hurt Andi based on the conversation I overheard at Brewed Bliss. The real tragedy is that this was all because Ava was jealous and insecure around Andi and all Andi wanted was to be Ava and Pixie's friend."

"With friends like that, you don't need any enemies," Luke said.

Mom asked, "So did Ava encourage Clark to make Andi sick?"

"In passing, Ava remarked wouldn't it be nice if Andi got the flu and couldn't go with them for a change. Pixie laughed and said it needed to be a two-week case of food poisoning.

For Clark, that was all it took to hatch his twisted plan. As a former smoker he knew that nicotine gum, if chewed too often, could make you feel sick, but he had no idea that chewing ten pieces of gum per day, or more, was deadly. Once Andi started to feel unwell, Clark thought she'd go home. But he underestimated her resilience. Here was a young woman who had spent her entire life not feeling up to par. To her, this was a minor distraction."

Gram frowned, "When did Ava realize what Clark had done?"

"She found the gum in Clark's suitcase and when she questioned him, he confessed why he did it."

Ethan nodded. "That was after Andi died or before?"

"After." My shoulders slumped. "Ava decided to protect her husband, and she was the one who stuffed the coat and shoulder bag in the shrubs—and it was Ava who saw me looking under them. She told Clark, who raced down the back stairs and waited for the perfect time to knock me out and take them."

Beth looked at Eddie. "Is Pixie innocent?"

"Of the crime, yes. Of being bad friend, no. I'm sure Hugo will be persona-non-grata once word gets out he's just a hanger-on to get the dirt on the wealthy. The part of him being in love with Andi won't matter. Pixie will go back to working at the resort while Ava and Clark will be prosecuted for their crimes."

Eddie hugged me from behind. "Even if Claudia isn't looking for clues, she gets the best information—and sharing it helped all the puzzle pieces fall into place."

I turned to look at him. "There's one question that's been bothering me."

"And that is?"

"How did you know to come to the inn? You were in the park with the others."

He scratched his cheek. "That's the darnedest thing. I was

questioning Hugo, and this blast of icy cold air went right through me. It seemed to move from my left to right and then it reversed. When I looked around to see what had happened, I could have sworn I saw a man who looked like the picture hanging in the lobby of the inn gesturing to me. Don't ask me why, but I followed him."

"You think you saw Thomas Pennington?" Gram asked.

"It must have been the stress of the situation, and on some level, I knew Claudia was in danger. I ran as fast as I could and met Rhonda getting in her cruiser. The rest you know."

Gram gave me a sly wink. It seemed Thomas could go farther than the property lines.

Mom announced, "Dinner's ready."

We gathered around the food-laden table. Ethan had Mom to his right and Gram to his left and Fiona was next to her. He took Mom's hand and kissed the back of it. "Thank you for making dinner tonight and I hope this is the beginning of a friends-and-family tradition. Sunday night dinners are a great way to kick off a new week."

Fiona beamed.

Mom smiled. "If you volunteer to do the dishes, I'll cook."

Luke and Beth sat next to each other, and she turned to me and Eddie. "I'm just sorry I missed out on all the action. The shop was so busy yesterday, which is great for the yarn business but not for sleuthing."

I laughed. "Not to worry Beth. There's always next time."

Are you ready to read more from Claudia and the gang in Drakes Bay?
Keep reading for a sneak peek of
Ribbons & Robbery
A Craft and Ghost Cozy Mystery
A Dress Designer Cozy Mystery Series

Order Now

Lucinda

Ribbons & Robbery

Enjoy this humorous, small-town, psychic, cozy mystery by best-selling and award-winning author, Lucinda Race.

She didn't want to talk to ghosts or investigate a murder.

The holidays are supposed to be magical, but when Claudia Grant's well-meaning grandmother signs her up—without asking—for a booth at the bustling Drakes Bay Holiday Market, things start to unravel like a dropped stitch in a knitting basket. Between hand-sewn Christmas and Hanukkah stockings, fabric wreaths, and a last-minute crash course in holiday bazaars, Claudia is in over her head—and that's before the local self-proclaimed influencer, Ginny Wicket, struts in with her designer brooches and bad attitude.

Claudia's ghostly Uncle Herman thinks Ginny's more trouble than tinsel, and he's rarely wrong. When petty squabbles turn sinister and a treasured vintage brooch disappears, suspicion runs as high as Ginny's heels. With Beth, her best friend and knitting guru, by her side—and a growing list of quirky townsfolk and committee cousins—Claudia must navigate ghostly advice, holiday mayhem, and a certain someone who just might be a little *too* obsessed with vintage sparkle.
Will Claudia survive her first holiday market… or will this festive event end in disaster?

Perfect for fans of crafty cozies, sassy sofa sleuths, and ghostly guidance with a touch of holiday cheer!

Ribbons & Robbery
A Craft and Ghost Cozy Mystery
A Dress Designer Cozy Mystery Series
Order Now

LUCINDA RACE

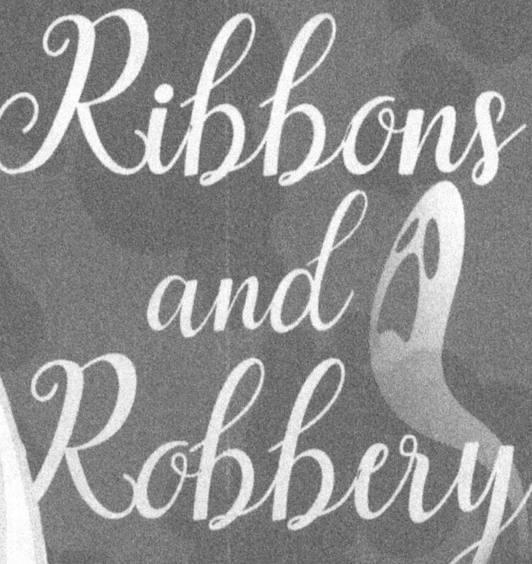

Ribbons
and
Robbery

A CRAFT AND GHOST COZY MYSTERY
A DRESS DESIGNER COZY MYSTERY SERIES
BOOK FOUR

CHAPTER ONE

Beth burst through the door to my dress shop with a wide grin, waving a slip of paper. "Claudia, I forgot to tell you. Erma signed you up to have a booth at the Drakes Bay Holiday Bazaar."

"My grandmother did what? A holiday market?" I snipped a thread from the label I'd attached to the Christmas stocking. It needed pressing, but I'd do that later.

After closing the door, she crossed to the counter. "Rut roh. Erma didn't tell you, did she?"

I held out my hand to Beth, my best friend and the owner of the local knitting shop across the street. "Nope. What's the story with the market, and do all shop owners participate?" I took a cursory look and set the paper aside.

"It's a craft bazaar, a holiday shopping extravaganza for folks to buy gifts. Since you're new in town you wouldn't know it's been a tradition in Drakes Bay for the last fifty years or so. My knitters all have tables with different items; one focuses on baby items, another on sweaters, and so on. They agree ahead of time what items they'll sell so they're not competing with each other."

At least that wouldn't be direct competition with my own

dress shop and the knitwear the local knitters supplied to me. "What am I supposed to sell? Dresses?"

She laughed. "No, silly, Christmas stockings. When Dana and Erma saw that your Uncle Herman tucked a tote in, they thought it would be a perfect way for more people in town to learn about Grants Gowns and you as the new owner. The event's popular with residents from Pembroke Cove and Robins Pointe. Lily Michaels's parents, Reed and Mindy, set up a tiny camper and sell tea."

Tipping my head, I thought, "I met them at her wedding. They're very nice."

"Just like Lily. Typically, she helps them out. She might even read tea leaves."

I picked up the next stocking and glanced at Beth. "We should plan a potluck dinner for after the bazaar. Maybe Lily's husband would drive down, and they could join us. It would be nice to get to know Lily better."

She nodded. "Great idea. I'll call Lily and ask her to ask Gage and her parents, too. Do you think you have enough stockings to sell? The sale is this Saturday."

My eyes bugged out. "What? I only have like twenty-five, and that was inventory for the rest of the month in the shop." I pushed back from the work table. "If it's busy, I could run out before lunch. What was Gram thinking? And when they left this morning, why didn't she mention it?"

Beth grinned as I slapped the stocking on the short stack. I asked, "What's so funny?"

"Erma said you'd have this reaction and to look in the red tote near the back entrance."

What had Gram gotten me into now? "What tote? There isn't a red one stored there."

"Go look." Beth turned me around and gave me a playful push from the stool.

With a flash of annoyance at Gran's latest *helpful* surprise, I glanced at Beth before striding the short distance to the door.

An oversized red tote, big enough to hide a body, well, at least my size, sat to the left of the door. Gran never did anything small. "Where did that come from?"

Beth bounced on her toes, looking entirely too pleased as a co-conspirator, "Open it."

She was awfully cheerful this morning. My brow arched, "Do you know what's in here?"

With a nod and a laugh, she said, "Don't make me repeat myself."

I flipped back the top. Stacked inside were Christmas stockings and Hanukkah stockings. "This is unbelievable." There had to be fifty, or more, stockings in the box.

"The Hanukkah stockings could be for blended families. Erma said some of her friends have them and thought they would be a great addition to your booth. As a bonus, your mom created fabric wreaths and placed them at the bottom. Bonus, you won't need to use the stockings you made for the store."

"They were plotting against me the entire time they were here for Thanksgiving?" I smacked my forehead. "They're unbelievable."

"As their partner in crime, I can assure you it was in a good way," Beth said.

I couldn't disagree with her, although I didn't want to admit it right now. Mom and Gram were always looking out for me.

Uncle Herman's ghost drifted into the workroom. "I see you've discovered Erma's handiwork?"

Although I wanted to answer my resident ghost, I couldn't while Beth was in the room. She had no idea I could talk to ghosts, and it might make her run back to her knitting store and never return.

A moment of panic gripped me. "Do you think I'll need more than what's here?"

With a wide smile that reassured me, as I exhaled.

"I don't," she said, "We'll share a booth space since this is your first year, and I'll have plenty of stuff to sell. If we get lucky and run out, we can do a bit of shopping ourselves."

She still held the paper in her hand. I nodded at it. "Do I have to fill that out?"

"No, your Gram took care of it, and she paid the entrance fee. The money goes to the Secret Santa fund."

"Which is?"

She snapped her fingers. "Right, you wouldn't know. We collect funds and unwrapped gifts for families in need across the county. Ginny Wicket, the event organizer, is thrilled that all the booths are filled."

"That's a name I haven't heard yet. Count me in, even if I don't sell a single item; helping kids is worth it." I grabbed a pen and jotted down to pick up some toys for the collection box. "What kind of toys should I bring?"

"Anything that looks fun to you." She pointed to the shelf of knit items. "While I'm here, I'll check inventory on our hat and scarf sets." She did a quick count and grinned. "You're almost sold out again. Our joint business venture seems to be doing well."

"It does." Beth and I had joined forces to enhance our businesses. She had knitters in town handcrafting items that complemented my clothing line. We'd only been working together for a couple of weeks, and so far it had been a huge success.

"I'm going out front to check on things," she said.

Once she was out of earshot, Herman drifted in as I sorted through the red tote. "I'm glad you're working the bazaar, but watch out for that Ginny Wicket. She's a piece of work. Bossy as all get out and likes telling everyone how to run their booths. Not friendly, either."

I whispered, "Did you do the bazaar?"

He perched on the edge of the work table. "No, I provided

stockings for Beth's table, and she donated all proceeds to the fund."

"Uncle Herman, that was sweet of you." I wished I could hug him, but my arms would slip through his vapor-like form.

"It's not a big deal, but to make it easier for you next year, you should make them over the coming months. Save scraps that will work, and Erma's idea of Hanukkah stockings is spot on. Also, they should make more wreaths like the ones your mom made. They'll be big sellers, especially if you do them in a variety of fabrics that span seasons."

Laughing, I shoved the tote back into the corner. "This is starting to sound like a side gig. How do you know so much about the wreaths and stockings?"

He winked. "Who do you think told Erma about the bazaar?"

I shook my head. "Are you and Gram conspiring against me?"

"Only for your benefit, Claudia. It's a great way to let others in the area know about Grants Gowns and your talent."

"I hardly think making holiday decorations will bring customers in the door, but it's a worthwhile endeavor, so I'll make you proud and continue the tradition."

Sliding from the table, he hovered next to me. "You always make me proud. The partnership with Beth was a stroke of genius."

"I can't take credit for the idea; it was all Beth. Marketing was my contribution."

He shook his head. "Don't discount what you did. Without the marketing, people wouldn't know about the new products except through word of mouth. And that would have taken forever to spread the news. Only gossip spreads fast in this small town."

Uncle Herman was right. "I have to get back to Beth."

He slipped through the door leading to my apartment, knowing I got squeamish when I walked through his translucent form by accident; on purpose, it would be even worse.

When I entered the front room, Beth was talking to a woman. Her voice had a defensive edge. "All booths are filled. What more do you want me to do?"

"Two words. Social media." The woman was closer to my mom's age, with short grey-blonde hair in an attractive bob, slender, and dressed in jeans and a black leather bomber jacket. "It's because of my online presence that Drakes Bay even gets visitors for the bazaar. Seaside areas like this are ghost towns from November until March. The town council should thank me for organizing this event."

"Ginny, there are a lot of people on the committee. I know there's an *I* in the word, but there's also a *T*, as in team."

It disturbed me to hear this woman attack Beth. I'd heard enough. "Beth, I'm glad you're still here." I walked to the woman and extended my hand. "Hello, welcome to Grants Gowns. I'm Claudia Grant, and you are?"

She took in my appearance from my toes to my ponytail. "Ginny Wicket." Reluctantly, she shook my hand and gestured to the sidewalk. "We're out wrapping up the last details for the event. Beth confirmed that you'll be joining us this year."

Giving her a warm smile, I said, "Yes, and I'm looking forward to it."

She looked down her nose. "Herman never attended but always gave a generous donation."

"So I've read. He kept extensive journals." I crossed my fingers behind my back and felt a coolness run over my hand. Herman was in the room.

He said, "Don't let her get under your skin. She's a pro at putting people on the defensive."

I straightened up and stood taller. "Beth and I will post on social media that we'll be at the bazaar. Hopefully, that helps draw in the knitting crowd. I've heard that previously, Uncle Herman also gave Beth stockings to sell in her booth. Shoppers might remember and come back."

Her lips pressed together, and her eyes narrowed. "My online presence will pull people in by the busload. I'm an influencer."

I cocked a brow. "Really? I'm sorry, but I don't recognize your name."

Ginny's mouth opened and closed like a goldfish's. To witness this woman at a loss for words was priceless. If I read her right, she thought highly of herself and less of us mere shopkeepers. "Will you have a booth?"

Her eyes widened, and she sniffed. "Of course. I have vintage-inspired brooches. Several blogs featured them for the Twelve Days of Christmas. I don't sell originals; they're worth thousands of dollars. I have costume copies for sale."

I gave her a professional smile. "I look forward to seeing them. Is there anything else Beth and I should be aware of before Saturday?"

"Who will keep your shop open for you?" Her gaze roamed the space.

I was surprised she asked the question. Surely it wasn't about my business. "I'll close for the day and reopen on Sunday. I don't want to shortchange the bazaar." I didn't want to miss this woman in action. It might be the most fun Beth and I'd have during the event, watching her strut around, puffing herself up.

She looked away and slipped her hands into her pockets. "When you're posting on the day of the event, make sure you include pictures not only of your booth but also of others. We want to draw in as many customers as possible."

Beth said, "Ginny, you can count on us."

Three women entered. Ginny frowned, "I told you to wait outside."

They exchanged nervous glances.

Beth smiled, "Ladies, have you met Claudia?"

I stepped forward and held out my hand. "Hello. Claudia Grant."

A woman stepped forward and clasped my hand. "I'm Bitsy Simonson, this is Fenna Stenson, Melissa Thorpe."

We shook hands. I smiled, "It's nice to meet everyone. You're all on the bazaar committee?"

Ginny frowned. "Supposedly."

Bitsy, tall and athletic, with long spiral auburn curls, laughed, "We try not to pay any attention to Ginny. She thinks she runs the world."

Fenna Stenson, a petite girl with ample curves and pin-straight dark hair, smiled. "I'm one of Beth's knitters. It's great to meet you. I'm thrilled that my sweaters are popular with your customers."

"Thanks, I am too." I turned to Melissa, wondering whether she, too, would rebuke Ginny's nastiness.

"I'm Melissa. I've seen you at the bank several times. I'm in the personal loan department."

"Are you ladies sisters?"

She beamed, "We're cousins, but as close as sisters. Bitsy's the youngest and tallest in the family; Fenna has the curves. I'm the blonde in the group, but we share facial features."

Instantly, I liked them. "It's wonderful to meet everyone. I just discovered I'll be selling stockings and wreaths at the event. I hope you'll stop by the booth Beth and I are sharing."

Fenna said, "You can count on us."

"Claudia," Ginny said, bringing the attention back to herself, "Remember to stop at my booth for a peek at the fabulous brooches. Who knows, it might inspire your next design."

Curiosity tugged at me. "Ginny, I can't wait to see your collection—it sounds intriguing."

Her eyes narrowed at Beth and me. "Set up begins at eight sharp, and the event opens at nine. Don't be late. We're professionals." She glanced at the cousins. "Well, most of us." Pivoting on her impossibly high-heeled boots, Ginny said, "Let's go, ladies. We have several stops before this meeting is concluded."

They followed her out the door, with each woman giving a small wave. Bitsy winked and flashed a cheeky grin before she closed the door.

I waited another minute and said, "Beth, did I get the wrong impression of Ginny, or does she think she's all that and a box of rocks? Meeting concluded. Who talks like that?"

Laughing, she asked, "What? You're asking if she can be insufferable? Heck yeah. But underneath, she's borderline intolerable. The only good thing I'll give her credit for is that she raises a lot of money for the holiday fund, so we put up with her for a couple of months out of the year."

I leaned against a display and looked at Ginny entering Brewed Bliss, the coffee shop across the street. "It's interesting she has an authentic vintage brooch collection."

"The really interesting point? She shows off the originals when someone is on the fence. I guess it's to highlight the quality of the costume piece. My favorite is the butterfly brooch, and Art Deco is my favorite period. I offered to buy it once, but she wouldn't sell it to me. I swear it was out of spite because she knew I wanted it. In a nutshell, if you see one you like, be super casual; otherwise, you'll be out of luck."

Glancing her way, I said, "I'll keep that in mind, but expensive jewelry isn't something I usually buy for myself. Now, let's talk about a few other details. Do we need a cash box, tissue, wrapping paper, or bags?"

Beth placed her hand on my shoulder. "Have you ever been to a holiday bazaar?"

I thought for a minute. "Maybe years ago. Why?"

"We'll have paper bags if needed, but most people bring tote bags or even rolling baskets and fill them up as they work their way around the booths. However, you could bring tissue paper to wrap around the stockings and wreaths."

"Good to know. What are you selling?" I looked at the tables and shelves with the knitted items.

She smiled, "*Begin to Knit* kits for kids and adults. I don't compete with other vendors who sell sweaters and such. This way, it's a win, and I'll have a new customer after a kit purchase."

I grinned. "You're going to sell out in no time—let's just hope nothing gets twisted at the bazaar."

**To keep reading Ribbons & Robbery
Order Now**

**A Craft and Ghost Cozy Mystery
A Dress Designer Cozy Mystery Series**

REVIEWS & NEWSLETTER

If You Loved Pleats & Poison
Leave a Review
Reviews help other readers discover books they'll love—and
they mean the world to authors.
If you enjoyed this story, please consider leaving a review.
Even a short review makes a difference.
Bookbub:
Goodreads:
Amazon
Barnes and Noble
Kobo
Apple Books
Google Play

Stay Connected with Lucinda
Join my reader community and be the first to hear about:
New releases
Subscriber-only specials
Bonus content and sneak peeks
Early access to upcoming books

I hope you want to keep up with my crazy antics of writing, gardening, cooking, and life with the pup.

Not ready to stop reading yet? If you sign up for my newsletter, you'll receive Cookies & Capers as my thank-you gift for choosing to get my newsletter.

This novella is only available by signing up for my newsletter

📬 Sign Up Here:
https://lucindarace.com/newsletter/
Thank you for being part of this journey!
— Lucinda

COZY MYSTERY BOOKS

All ebooks and paperback copies can be ordered from my website at:
Shop at Lucinda Race

A Bookstore Cozy Mystery Series
Book 1 — Books & Bribes
Book 2 — Catnaps & Crimes
Book 3 — Tea & Trouble\
Book 4 — Scares & Dares
Book 5 — Holidays & Homicide
Book 6 — Leprechauns & Larceny
Book 7 - Magicians & Murder
Book 8 — Artifacts & Amulets
Book 9 — Cranberries & Criminals
Book 10— Broomsticks & Blooms
Book 11 Fishing & Forgery
Book 12 — Weddings & Wands
Book 13 — Covens & Clues

Dress Designer Cozy Mystery Series
Book 1 — Ghosts & Gowns

Book 2 — Buttons & Burglary
Book 3 — Pleats & Poison
Book 4 — Ribbons & Robbery

Temperance Matthews Cozy Mystery Series
Book 1 — Just Desserts & Murder
Book 2 — Cupcakes & Murder
Book 3 — Walnut Brownies & Murder
Book 4 - Coming Soon

Witches of Robins Pointe
A Paranormal Cozy Mystery Series
Inherited Magic & Murder 2027
Touch of Magic February 2027
Waiting for Magic March 2027

Visit Lucinda Online
Website: www.lucindarace.com
Join the Newsletter: https://lucindarace.com/newsletter/

ROMANCE BOOKS

**All ebooks and paperback copies can be ordered from my website at:
website at:
Shop at Lucinda Race**

Small-Town Romance
The Price Family Romance Series
Book 1 — Breathe
Book 2 — Crush
Book 3 — Blush
Book 4 — Vintage
Book 5 — Bouquet
Book 6 — *Cantina* November 2026
Price Family Romance Boxset

The McKenna Family Romance Series
Book 1 — Lost and Found
Love never ends... A widow who talks to her husband's ghost and her handsome single neighbor who has secretly loved her for years.
Book 2 — The Journey Home
Book 3 — The Last First Kiss
Book 4 — Ready to Soar

Book 5 — Love in the Looking Glass
Book 6 — Magic in the Rain
Book 7 — After All These Years
McKenna Family Romance Boxset

The MacLellan Sisters Romance Series
Book 1 — Old and New
Book 2 — Borrowed
Book 3 — Blue
MacLellan Sisters Trilogy

Cowboys of River Junction
Contemporary Western Cowboy Romance Series
Book 1 — Second Chances in Montana
Book 2 — Stars Over Montana
Book - 3 Hiding in Montana
Book - 4 Moonlight Over Montana
Cowboys of River Junction Boxset

Sunsets of New England Romance Series
Book 1 — The Matchmaker and The Marine
Book 2 — Shamrocks Are A Girl's Best Friend
Book - 3 Love, Weddings & Second Chances - A Collection
Book - 4 Holiday Hearts - A Collection
Book - 5 Holly Berries & Hockey Pucks
Book - 6 A Secret Santa Christmas

ABOUT THE AUTHOR

Award-winning and best-selling author Lucinda Race has been captivated by stories for as long as she can remember. A lifelong reader who fell head over heels for cozy mysteries and heartfelt romances as a young girl, she now brings that same magic to her own books.

Stories Filled with Heart, Hope, and a Hint of Mystery
Although her writing career began in nonfiction, storytelling always called her back home. Today, she delights readers with the beloved McKenna Family Romance series and the Paranormal Cozy Nook Bookstore Series—creating charming small towns, lovable characters, and page-turning mysteries filled with heart.

Whether crafting a swoon-worthy romance or a twisty cozy mystery, Lucinda writes the kinds of stories she loves to read —stories that leave readers smiling long after the final page.

Now with over 40 books published, she's living her dream and loves connecting with readers at LucindaRace.com.

SOCIAL MEDIA

Follow Me on Social Media

Like my Facebook page
Join Lucinda's Heart Racer's Reader Group on Facebook
Twitter @lucindarace
Instagram @lucindaraceauthor
BookBub
Goodreads
Pinterest
YouTube